The ZEE FILES

All that Glitters

The
ZEE FILES
All that Glitters

BY TINA WELLS

with Stephanie Smith
Illustrated by Mike Segawa

WEST
MARGIN
PRESS

For Quorra. My biggest inspiration.
I love you more than anything else in the world. —S.S.

Written with Stephanie Smith
Illustrated by Mike Segawa

ISBN: 9781513277349

Printed in Canada

24 23 22 21 2 3 4 5

Published by West Margin Press

**WEST
MARGIN
PRESS**
WestMarginPress.com

WEST MARGIN PRESS
Publishing Director: Jennifer Newens
Marketing Manager: Angela Zbornik
Project Specialist: Micaela Clark
Editor: Olivia Ngai
Design & Production: Rachel Lopez Metzger

1

FAMILY REUNION

"Zee, darling, breakfast is ready!" Mrs. Carmichael called.
Mackenzie Blue Carmichael turned over in her bed on the third floor of her London home and looked toward the window, searching for her cell phone to check the time. Her hand whacked against the nightstand, knocking over her journal, but she caught her phone before it could fall to the ground too. The oversized numbers on the screen read 7:15 a.m. Zee had looked forward to sleeping in a bit longer than she would back on campus at The Hollows Creative Arts Academy, but alas, between the twins rising at sunup and her father's early schedule, the whole house had been dressed and ready for the day for the past hour.

Zee sat up in bed and looked at her phone with tired eyes. A message had come in from Ally, her BFF currently living in Paris. It was a copy of the train schedule from London to Paris for the next week.

Ally and Zee have been best friends since they both lived in California and attended the same grade school, Brookdale

Academy. Ally moved to Paris a few years ago, and Zee just moved to London at the end of summer after her father took a new job. Zee and Ally planned to meet up in Paris this week while Zee was on fall break—Ally's parents recently split up, and she could use some cheering up from her bubbly and energetic friend Zee.

Let me check and see which day will work! Zee texted back. She was excited to make this trip happen, especially since Ally had canceled on her when they scheduled their first reunion in Paris right before school started.

Zee threw back the covers, swung her legs off the edge of the bed, and sat up. She stretched her arms overhead and rose to her tippy toes before relaxing her heels back down to the

floor. It was her first night's sleep back in her London home since she went off to boarding school. There was something so comforting about her old bed, the way the worn-in mattress hugged her body and the softness of her favorite flannel sheets.

Her bed at The Hollows Creative Arts Academy, the boarding school she transferred to at the beginning of the school year, was comfortable but not yet familiar. But it didn't matter—by the time her head hit the pillow at night, Zee was so exhausted from the day as a new year nine student that she could fall asleep on any flat surface.

The schoolwork was challenging. Whether it was the language differences or the teaching styles, Zee found it hard to concentrate on the lectures. She was hoping her parents wouldn't ask how her grades were. Why ruin a great week home with disappointing news?

Luckily, making new friends has been easier than making high marks. Zee's roommate, Jameela Chopra, was a sharp and intellectual ballet dancer who showed Zee the ropes of boarding school, though she had high standards for herself and everyone else. Izzy Matthews, a popular year nine student thanks to her YouTube channel with 50,000 followers, invited Zee to her study group, then to her Cotswolds family estate for a sleepover. Zee also has her friend Jasper Chapman, who attended Brookdale Academy for a year until he returned to London this past summer. He was the only person Zee knew in London before her first day at school.

And then there was Archie Saint John. Mysterious guy on campus. Talented guitarist. Few friends, but lives a very posh life. Zee met Archie on the first day of school after she ran into him—literally—on the quad. The two had hit it off over their music interests, and Archie invited Zee to a few jam sessions to work on their performances for the Creative Arts Festival coming up near the end of fall term. He paid Zee more attention than he did to anyone else at school. Maybe they were just friends. Or maybe more? Zee has spent more hours trying to figure out what's really going on between her and Archie than she has on her studies. As of now, she has neither the grades nor a label to describe her thing with Archie to show for her time.

Knock knock knock! "Zee, honey, would you like me to make you something to eat?"

Camilla, the Carmichael family's new nanny, was waiting for a response on the other side of the door. Zee's eyes widened as she turned her head. She thought to open the door and face Camilla directly, which would be the polite thing to do. But to Zee, Camilla still felt like a stranger, even though she'd been taking care of her family members since the school year began. Zee couldn't let a stranger see her with morning breath and crazy bed head.

"Um, I'll be down in a minute. I can grab something then," Zee replied. She waited for Camilla's footsteps to fade away, then headed to the restroom, brushed her teeth, washed her face, and got dressed for the day.

• • •

The kitchen of the Carmichael family's Notting Hill residence smelled like coffee and sounded like a train station. Phoebe and Connor, Zee's twin siblings, waddled across the floor, following their mother as she looked for a serving plate.

Mr. Carmichael took a few sips of coffee while checking his e-mails on his phone. "Looks like I have a meeting at 5 p.m. Might be a bit late home tonight," he warned anyone within earshot.

"Okay, darling," Mrs. Carmichael responded. She fluttered past her husband and gave him a kiss on the cheek before she breezed toward the pantry. "I've got a meetup with the girls today."

"The girls as in your daughters?" he asked.

"No, the girls as in the Mummy Mums," Mrs. Carmichael said.

"Who?" Zee asked as she walked up behind her mother. Her father looked back at his phone.

Mrs. Carmichael explained, "They're my new mom friends. I met them at a park a few weeks ago while I was out with the twins. They all live close by and have young children, and they plan playdates and outings. They're very connected too. One of them, Sophie, sat next to me on a bench and helped me get Phoebe settled when she was fussy. She was so lovely. She introduced me to her friends, and now I'm sort of part of the circle."

"You get together every day with them?" Zee asked, sitting down at the kitchen table. "And the kids too?"

"Not every day, and not always with the kids."

"I've never met these new friends, honey," Mr. Carmichael chimed in.

"Well, you will," Mrs. Carmichael responded.

Zee looked at her mom. Her mother's curly hair, usually left long and loose in California, was tied into a low bun and smoothed back with a printed silk scarf. She wore a beautifully tailored gray tea-length dress and a tall pair of boots. In California, her mother had lived in vintage T-shirts and cut-off shorts, or long, wide-legged linen pants and sneakers. She sure has adapted to her London surroundings, Zee thought.

Mrs. Carmichael grabbed a large platter from the bottom pantry shelf and handed it to Camilla, then walked to the sitting nook where Zee was enjoying her breakfast. Mrs. Carmichael leaned over the cup of coffee she was holding with two hands. "And what's on your agenda today, Zee?"

Zee looked down at the plate of eggs, perfectly browned toast and jam, and sliced fruits Camilla had artfully arranged for her. "Probably a little more of this," she responded.

"Well, darling, I was hoping we could do something fun together while you were here. You know, maybe some shopping or a nice lunch somewhere in town."

Zee looked at her mother, whose British accent had become so much more pronounced in the few weeks Zee's been gone. "Ally texted me last night and said she does want to meet up in Paris now. Did you know her parents were splitting up?"

"No, really?" her father said. "That's a shame."

"Yeah, I think her mother is back in California," Zee said. "Anyway, can I go to Paris this week to meet up with her?"

Mr. Carmichael made his way toward the door. "I can't do it this week, Zee. I'm on a shoot for a new campaign that I have to oversee."

Mrs. Carmichael perked up. "Zee, maybe we should go together! We can leave the twins with Camilla and you and I can have a girls trip."

Zee couldn't remember the last time she hung out with her mother alone since the twins arrived. While she appreciated her mother's offer, Zee was more excited to connect with Ally about important things, like how Ally was getting along with her dad, and how Zee was getting along with school—and, most importantly, Archie.

"I haven't seen Ally in so long. We have so much to catch up on," Zee said.

"I understand," Mrs. Carmichael said. "Tell you what, I'll take you to Paris and then give you and Ally some space to hang out. I'll sit at a different table at the restaurant or something. And then we can shop and come back home. Ooh, there's that amazing macaron shop we can check out while we're there. Sound good?"

Quality time with her best friend in Paris. Mom as a socially distanced chaperone. And macarons? "I'm in!" Zee said.

2

PARIS PART DEUX

Zee texted her pal Ally bright and early on Wednesday, the day they'd agreed to meet in Paris.

Zee

> Good morning! You ready for today? Don't bail on me this time!

Ally didn't delay in her response.

Ally

> I'm already up and getting ready. Can't wait to see you! #parispartdeux

Zee jumped out of bed, excited to get her day started. She picked out an outfit for her visit the night before—a black-and-white striped T-shirt and a black ankle-length knit skirt with a denim jacket. Zee assumed she should know enough French to be able to ask for the train, a restroom, and a croissant, so she clicked the Rosetta Stone app on her phone and listened while she got ready. *"Où sont les toilettes?"* she repeated along with the voice recording.

Zee went down for breakfast, skipping over to her twin siblings to give them a snuggle before grabbing some toast and jam. Camilla was helping Mrs. Carmichael feed the twins, who were dressed in matching knit sweatpants and baby vintage T-shirts. Shoeboxes and shopping bags lay at the foot of the twins' high chairs. Small jars of baby food and used baby wipes were scattered on their food trays.

"All right, now that the little ones are fed, dressed, and photographed, I'm going to get dressed myself," Mrs. Carmichael said, her phone in her hand.

"What time do we need to leave?" Zee asked.

"In twenty minutes. I'll be ready, don't worry."

After Zee devoured her breakfast, she packed a few snacks, her headphones, and her tablet into her backpack and left it by the door. While Camilla did the dishes, Zee got down on the floor with her toddler siblings, playing peekaboo until her mother came back down the stairs.

Mrs. Carmichael looked straight out of the pages of *Vogue Paris*, with her hair pulled back into a low bun and dark sunglasses on her face, wearing a white off-the-shoulder top with a pair of slim black slacks. "I'm ready. We'll take an Uber to the train, right? Camilla, we'll be back around dinnertime."

Zee watched her mother plant kisses on Phoebe's and Connor's foreheads and head toward the front door. She looked at Camilla, then at her mom, then back at Camilla, wondering if the new nanny really knew everything about the kids that she should. Does she know that Connor refused to sleep on his back or without his favorite stuffed animal, Mr. Whiskers? Or about Phoebe's disdain for green leafy vegetables?

"Zee, let's go, we're going to be late," Mrs. Carmichael called.

Zee shook her head, grabbed her backpack and shoes, and followed her mother into the Uber waiting in front of their house. She looked back at the twins, happily crawling toward Camilla who sat on the floor with a few soft picture books and brightly colored toys.

. . .

On the train ride to Paris, Mrs. Carmichael spent most of the time staring at her phone, texting Camilla about the twins' whereabouts, editing photos, and responding to DMs from her social media followers. At one point, Mrs. Carmichael spoke into her phone as she recorded the view of the British countryside as the train zoomed by. "We are headed to Pariiiiiiiiisssss!" she said, leaning toward Zee. Zee looked up and smiled for a selfie with her mother while making a peace sign with her right hand.

On her own phone, Zee looked through photos and messages from Ally and Chloe. *I'm so jealous you guys get to hang, but also so happy you get to see each other. Send picccccs!* Chloe texted the group last night, which Ally and Zee received this morning given the time differences between California, London, and Paris.

Two hours later, Zee and her mother arrived in Paris and headed for the 7th arrondissement. ("*Arrondissement* is a French word for 'district,'" Mrs. Carmichael had explained to Zee the night before when Ally texted where they should meet.) Ally suggested going to her favorite coffee shop where she went almost every day after school. *They have the. Best. Croissants*, Ally wrote. She and her father had already arrived at the restaurant a few minutes earlier and were waiting for the Carmichaels at a back table.

Zee walked into Le 29, a classic French bistro with several tables outside and a glass door that opened to a small dining room with a dozen or so tables. She scanned the room for Ally. There was a young-looking girl sitting in the corner with an older gentleman who looked just like Mr. Stern. The girl, dressed in black and wearing a berry shade of lip gloss, looked at Zee. "You made it!" Ally said.

"*Ohmylanta!* Ally! I missed you so much!" Zee squealed as she looked at her best friend. "Wow, Ally, you look so grown up!"

"Oh, thanks," Ally said shyly. "Hi, Mrs. Carmichael."

"Ally, so good to see you! How are you doing?" Mrs. Carmichael said, hugging her, then gave a polite nod to Mr. Stern, who slowly rose from his seat to greet Ally's guests.

"I'm so glad you both made the trip. How is everything in London?" he asked.

"It's great," Mrs. Carmichael replied. "Rainy weather, but Zee being home from break makes things a bit sunnier."

"Aw, Mom!" Zee said, her cheeks turned a bashful shade of red.

Mr. Stern smiled, then planted a kiss on Ally's left cheek. "Text when you're ready. I'll meet you here." Ally nodded and turned toward Zee.

"I'll keep an eye on them but still give them some space to

gossip," Mrs. Carmichael said. "Ladies, I might sit at another table and make a phone call after we order to give you two some time. Is that all right?"

"Thanks, Mom," Zee said.

"Great. Then we can do a little shopping."

Mrs. Carmichael walked toward the middle of the dining room while Ally and Zee sat down at the table. "You still seem different," Zee said. "Have you been wearing makeup since you got here?"

"No, but I put on a red lip gloss for special occasions. Just a little something. French women have perfected that no-makeup makeup thing, so wearing a bunch of stuff on my face wouldn't be cool here."

A server swooped in and stood by their table. He placed menus down in front of them and rattled off a few short sentences in French. Ally said, "They have the best burgers here. I know, surprising for a French place, but their burgers and fries are just as good as their croissants."

"Then let's get both!" Zee said.

Ally ordered for both of them in conversational French. "*Deux hamburgers frites, s'il vous plaît, deux pains au chocolat, et un croissant, s'il vous plaît.*"

"Can you also order some tea?" Zee asked.

"*Et un thé?*" Ally added.

"*Oui,*" the server replied with a serious look. "*C'est tout?*"

"*Oui.*"

When he left, Zee turned to her friend and put her hand on her shoulder. "So, how are you really?"

Ally shook her head. "I'm okay. It's just horrible about my parents. But I guess maybe I saw it coming? They did fight a lot. Not like with fists, but they just argued all the time. They couldn't agree on a pizza order. So I guess I'm not surprised."

Zee listened and shook her head. She looked over at her mother on the phone and tried to think back to the last time her parents ordered takeout. It was pretty drama-free, though she remembered her mom having to remind her dad to grab extra napkins.

Ally continued. "Anyway, my mom moved out over the summer and went to live in another part of town. I think she's planning to move back to the States because I've heard her talking on the phone a lot to my aunt who lives back in California. Mom recently went back there for a week to visit her. I don't know what's going to happen."

"Whoa," Zee said. "How's your dad?"

"He just works all the time."

"So is it just you and him in the house most of the time?"

"Yeah. But I have the literary journal and meetings for that after school most days, so we end up coming home around the same time." Ally had joined a literary journal where she wrote a column about her life as an American girl in Paris.

"But do you guys, like, do stuff together?"

"Lately we've been going to more museums and out to eat and stuff," Ally said. She picked nervously at her cuticles. "There have been a few cool exhibits we've seen together. But I do the shopping and fun stuff with my mom. Sometimes my dad and I go to the river and walk around on the weekends. That's fun. Sometimes."

The server returned with plates of burgers and fries, croissants, teacups, and small pots of fresh preserves. He then went over to Zee's mom's table and placed a salad in front of her. The croissants were warm to the touch. The girls bit into each one, Ally happy to be eating and not thinking about her parents. Zee noticed a difference between California Ally and Paris Ally—Cali Ally was carefree and giggly, even when she had braces. Paris Ally was more sullen and serious, understandably so given her parents' divorce. But also more refined—hence the red lip gloss.

"But what's going to happen for the holidays? Will you do Christmas together?" Zee asked.

"I don't know. Last year we did it here and then my father left for a work trip right after."

Zee thought back to her holidays last year. The twins were about a year old, so Zee's dad dressed up like Santa Claus to bring them presents. There was hot chocolate around the firepit in the backyard and her mom had s'mores and homemade cookies. Her brother Adam was home from college too, and the entire family hung out in matching plaid pajamas for what seemed like the entire Christmas break.

"These croissants are amazing," Zee said.

"Right? They're like comfort food for me," Ally said, placing her pastry onto the small plate in front of her and picking up the burger with two hands. "But right, let's talk about London. How's school? Have you seen Jasper?"

"Yes, he's been great. Though I haven't heard from him during fall break, which is a bit weird. London is interesting. School is fine. Lots of great people. Lots of hard schoolwork."

"Are you working on music?"

"Yeah. Actually, there's a big arts festival at the end of fall term that most of the students participate in, so I'll likely perform in that."

"Really?" Ally said. "Like a solo?"

Zee paused upon hearing the word "solo." It was the first time she'd thought about what performing without her Beans music mates meant: her on a stage alone with no support. "I guess," she said slowly.

"Cool. You were always a great lead singer when we were with The Beans. Is Jasper helping you, or that other guy you had the text date with?"

"Archie," Zee said. "Yeah, Archie has given me some chords to work with. I guess I could ask him to perform with me... maybe... if I wanted to. But I haven't thought that through."

Mrs. Carmichael approached the table and told the girls she was going to take a call outside and to sit tight.

Ally watched as Mrs. Carmichael walked away. "So does your mom know about this Archie?"

"No, no one knows about this Archie, except for you and Chloe. Jasper assumes something's going on, but really there's not... I mean, I don't think. But Archie did kiss me."

"What?" Ally said, leaning back and putting her hand to her mouth. "You didn't tell me that earlier."

"Sorry! Yeah, he kissed me on the cheek after one of our music sessions. It was shocking really. But, like, it could have just been friendly. It's hard to tell with him."

"Have you seen him since?"

"No. That was right before fall break, and I haven't heard from him." Zee chewed on her fries slowly, thinking to herself. "I haven't heard from Jasper either."

The girls laughed and joked as they scarfed down their lunches, comparing the burgers to the ones they had at the diner in their old California neighborhood. "I don't eat a lot of meat, but when I do I want it to be the best burger or sandwich or steak out there," Zee said. "This is definitely worth eating meat for."

Just as they finished, Mrs. Carmichael came back inside and approached Ally and Zee's table. "Girls, ready for some street fashion? Or just fashion?"

"Sure, Mom," Zee said, rolling her eyes. Ally giggled at Mrs. Carmichael's joke.

Mrs. Carmichael paid the bill at the register near the front entrance, and the girls gathered their things. The three of them spilled out onto the sidewalk, then walked toward the Eiffel Tower to get a photo in front of the iconic structure. "Ooooh, this is a great photo," Mrs. Carmichael cooed.

Ally and Zee's eagerly snapped their own selfies in front of the tower. They smiled, giggled, then did a few dance moves in front of the landmark, and texted a photo to Chloe with the caption: *Wish you were here!*

As they headed toward the river, Mrs. Carmichael pointed her phone back at herself as she walked by a beautifully decorated townhouse with French doors and flower boxes. "Ooh, this is another good one!" she said as she walked past a patisserie with three older French women sitting outside smoking cigarettes.

Mrs. Carmichael wrestled to get something out of her oversized purse. A long silver wand unfolded in her hand with a small plastic phone case. Mrs. Carmichael slipped the phone in the case and extended the phone away from her, snapping photos with a click of the button on the stick.

"Mom, a selfie stick in Paris? You're such a tourist!" Zee said.

Mrs. Carmichael smiled and filmed the girls while they walked along. Zee, embarrassed, put her hand to the side of her face.

They popped into a boutique with thin white mannequins wearing designer clothes in the window. Ally and Zee quickly surveyed the racks of clothes, but Mrs. Carmichael carefully palmed every item she passed by, oohing and ahhing along the way as she shopped. She tried on a stack of dresses and outfits at one store that, between the wardrobe changes including shoe swaps and the pictures taken, took a half hour.

"Cashmere really is your mom's thing, huh?" Ally said.

"Likes are her new thing," Zee said. "She's obsessed. Before she had the twins, she barely even texted. Now she spends all her time on Instagram and TikTok. It's annoying."

The girls walked toward the jackets and Mrs. Carmichael swooped in behind them, running her hands over a cropped leather jacket with silver studs. "Ooh, this feels amazing. And Priscilla will love it."

"Who's Priscilla?" Zee asked.

"My friend from Mummy Mums. She's so stylish. I'm going to try it on."

Mrs. Carmichael moved in front of a nearby mirror and tried on the jacket, taking selfies and making duck-lipped faces toward the camera. Ally giggled while she watched. Zee cringed.

Ally smiled at Mrs. Carmichael and Zee's banter. She looked at her friend's grumpy face. "At least your mother is here," Ally said. She missed happy antics with her own mother. She missed a lot of things with her own mother.

"Girls, we should hustle," Mrs. Carmichael said. "We still

have to make it to Ladurée before we have to head back to the train station."

They filed out to the street once again, walking toward Champs-Élysées so they could get a photo in front of the Arc de Triomphe in the distance. A few minutes later, they arrived at Ladurée, the famed bakery chain and producer of the best macarons in the world. Zee and Ally looked over the assortment of fresh desserts through the glass case and chose several flavors of macarons based on their vibrant colors—purple was for a lavender flavor, while a pale-green shade tasted like mint. Zee and Mrs. Carmichael picked out a few macarons for the family back at home and carried them in a beautiful box, one among the many boxes Mrs. Carmichael had acquired from her shopping spree throughout the day.

As the group returned back to Le 29, Ally texted her dad they were on their way. They enjoyed the view of the people and the bustling street life until they finally reached the cozy restaurant again. Mr. Stern met them outside a few minutes afterward. Ally's face softened into boredom, dreading the return trip back to their apartment where her father would spend the rest of the night hunched over his laptop computer while Ally was left to entertain herself.

Ally hugged Zee tightly and took a deep breath. "Thank you so much for coming. This was so great."

"For sure. We could do this more often. It's only two hours away!"

"Yeah," Ally said, a twinge of sadness in her words. "You're so lucky, Zee. You still have your mom. She might be busy or obsessed with influencing. But... she's there."

"I know," Zee said. "She is certainly around. Call me more

often, Ally. You know we can talk about anything. If you need me, I am here. I miss you."

"I will," Ally said. "I'm sorry I've been so distant."

"I get it," Zee said. "I'll put our photos from today in our Zee Files."

The two friends hugged each other tightly again, then Mr. Stern's cell phone rang loudly in the restaurant. "Oh, Ally, we better go. I have to prep for a call later."

Ally shook her head and walked backwards away from Zee. The Sterns then quickly turned toward the metro station, fading into the masses of people milling about the city. Zee smiled, happy to have finally reunited and reconnected with her good friend. It was as if she had returned to her old happy life in California, even just for an afternoon.

• • •

Zee and her mother arrived back at their home in London with their arms heavy with shopping bags from their daylong jaunt in Paris. Camilla came to the front entrance to help them carry the bags inside, the three of them looking like a circus act as they meandered through the door.

Mr. Carmichael looked confused. "Did you buy out all of Paris?" he joked.

"I tried," Mrs. Carmichael said. She put the bags in a heap by the kitchen counters, and Camilla stacked them neatly. The twins shuffled around Mrs. Carmichael's legs, excited to see what treats their mother brought home for them.

Zee slinked back to her room, relieved to remove herself from the commotion. *What happened to my mother,* she wondered. *She's got a whole new wardrobe. She's obsessed with documenting her every move. It's as if my mother is now a full. Blown. Influencer.*

Flopping onto her bed, Zee dug her phone out of her bag and logged onto her computer. She opened the folder on her home screen titled "The Zee Files," a private, invite-only file where she, Ally, and Chloe uploaded documents, pictures, and audio and video files to share. The Zee Files was like a virtual interactive scrapbook, and an easy way to keep in touch for three girls living across eight time zones.

Zee looked through the photos on her phone from today's trip, including a selfie with Ally at the burger joint and a nice photo of them together in front of the Eiffel Tower. She opened

the file on her computer to upload the photos, but noticed that someone had left a few new messages. In a new folder called "Paris, Zee, and Me," Ally had already uploaded her photos of her and Zee in front of the Eiffel Tower and on Champs-Élysées, with a caption: *My best friend. No matter how far apart we are, we always have each other.*

3

THE ZEN DEN

A week at home and a visit to see her best friend was just what Zee needed to feel refreshed and revived enough to go back to school. That and some home cooking of course, even if Camilla, instead of her mother, now made most of the meals.

Zee packed up her bags, saving room for fresh laundry and a few of the macarons left over from Ladurée. Mr. Carmichael arranged to take Zee back to school after missing picking her up last week because of a meeting. Zee hopped into the SUV with her father to head back to The Hollows, about an hour's drive away.

As Zee and her father got settled in the SUV, Zee's phone vibrated in her purse. She fished it out, wondering who it could be.

It was a message from Archie.

Archie

> Hey, Cali. On your way back to school?

Zee hadn't heard from him all week. She began to write him back, smiling with each word, when her father piped up. "So, how is school going?"

"It's fine. Better than I thought it would be," Zee blurted, flipping her phone face down to hide it from her father.

"Yeah? Good to hear. I want to make sure you feel okay there."

"I feel fine," Zee said. "My roommate is okay, though very intense. I've made some other friends though. And music is a lot of fun. We're learning about jazz now in music theory, Dad. Your favorite."

"Nice," Mr. Carmichael said. "Have you been performing with anyone? Think you'll start another band on campus?"

"No, not another band. I can't replace my Beans," Zee said. She hesitated about telling her father about Archie. It seemed too complicated to explain. "For now, I'm just writing. I'll probably do something for the Festival next month."

"Oh that's right, the Arts Festival! That's big, right? We'll make sure to be there."

Zee nodded, then looked back at her phone. She continued typing a response to Archie.

Zee

> Hey. How was your week? I'm just driving back to campus.

Archie

> Fine. Played some songs, but music sounds better with you, Cali.

Zee's face felt flush with anticipation.

Are you headed back to school?

Archie

I'll be back tomorrow. Got a family thing here mañana. Can't wait to hear what you've been working on. Jam session this week?

Zee smiled in the passenger seat and held the phone close to her chest.

• • •

When Zee returned to her dorm room, Jameela was sitting on the bed, her long, thin legs extended in front of her and crossed at the ankles, and a magazine sprawled out on top of them. She had on a sheet mask over her face and her long, dark hair was loosely tied up into a bun. Zee had never seen Jameela look so relaxed.

"Hiiiii," Zee said as she rolled her bags through the door.

"Hello," Jameela replied softly, as if she were dreaming.

"Wow, it seems like you got a lot of work done while I was gone. "

"I danced for six hours today," Jameela said. "My legs and feet were in such pain afterward. I had to massage them out. Then I thought, why not treat my entire body to something nice? Every girl needs some time for self-care, you know."

"Do I smell coconut oil?"

"It's in my hair. A little deep conditioner."

Zee dropped her overnight bag on her bed and sat down.

She took off her jacket and leaned back on her own bed, taking a breather before unpacking.

"Have you had dinner yet?" Zee asked.

"No, I had a big lunch after ballet. I might just grab something downstairs after my hair is done. They're having a bit of a Sunday roast down there. Roast beef, potatoes, Yorkshire pudding. Traditional British Sunday dinner fare."

"Yeah we had an early dinner at my house before I came back to school. I brought a few things back." Zee opened her bag and pulled out a small box of leftover macaroons. She

placed the box in front of Jameela's legs. "These will make you feel amazing, trust me."

After putting her clean clothes in her drawers and closet and unpacking the rest of her toiletries, Zee turned on her laptop and pulled up her schedule for the next few days. The anxiety kicked in fast and furious.

Zee looked up from the computer and slumped in her desk chair. Her palms became sweaty and she bit her upper lip. "I have to study."

"Right now?" Jameela said. "It's Sunday night. What's so pressing to study now? Surely none of your teachers were so cruel as to assign a test for tomorrow?"

"This from the girl already getting straight A's in all of her classes," Zee replied.

"I did get some studying done during the week. Did you take your books home?"

"Some of them."

"And did you read any of them while you were gone?"

"Well, I planned to, but then I was, um... busy."

"Right."

"I went to Paris with my mom to visit my best friend."

"Oh, that sounds lovely," Jameela said, biting into a mint-flavored macaron. "But that does not sound like a great place to study."

"It was a great place to shop and get those macarons you're so enjoying."

Jameela opened one eye behind her face mask. "Right."

Zee looked at her schedule for tomorrow. After Monday assembly, she had algebra (eek!), then sciences with Jasper and Izzy (fun, but also eek!), then a morning break before

English, where she knew that Mrs. Pender would ask her if Zee finished the reading assignment she assigned over break, and Zee would have to say, "Almost!" Which was, in fact, true. Then there was her Skills for Life class, intro to art history, and music theory with Archie.

Zee shook her head. "I can't take this."

"What's up?"

Zee slammed her laptop shut. "This is a lot."

Jameela took the face mask off and sat up from her pillow. "Zee, I worked very hard to get this chill. Don't kill my vibe."

Zee slumped onto her bed. She looked at Jameela. Before Zee had left for home, Jameela was the one who was stressed out, solely focused on ballet, not sleeping, and staying up late to practice. Now she was the picture of zen. How did she do it? "What can I do to relax then?" Zee asked.

Jameela slung her legs around to face Zee. She looked at her roommate and thought it might be the first time since term started that Zee wasn't smiling. "I think you need to meditate. Or do something that reminds you you're doing okay. I have to say, Tom was the one who inspired me to meditate."

"Really?"

"Yeah, but don't tell him that. I don't want to inflate his ego any more. Anyway, there are a few great apps out there that can guide you through a practice."

"I've never meditated before," Zee said. "Is it hard?"

"No. You literally sit there and breathe. Couldn't be easier."

"That's all?" Zee asked.

"And you bring your focus to your body and the breath, and let go of anything that is stressful or negative. It's helped me one hundred percent."

"How long do I have to do it for?"

"As long as you want. Until you feel better, I suppose. Want to try it now?"

Jameela showed Zee the mediation app on her phone that she used frequently and walked her through a few breathing techniques. "Just breathe in through your nose and out through your nose, and let your breath be natural and even." Then Jameela left the room to wash the rest of the face mask off her face, leaving Zee alone in the room.

"Breathe in, breathe out," Zee repeated to herself. She clicked open one of the meditations on the app and listened to the dreamy voice narrating soft commands. Zee followed the directions, letting go of anything that wasn't related to relaxing.

Five minutes later, Jameela returned to the room and found Zee fast sleep in her bed, her headphones resting over her ears and the dreamy voice from the phone still speaking soft instructions into Zee's ears.

4

SCHOOL'S IN SESSION

*A*fter assembly, Zee hummed to herself as she walked across the campus quad toward her classes. The melody had been in her head for weeks, ever since Archie played it for her in one of their private jam sessions. His guitar riffs matched the beginning of her song about lost connections perfectly, as if somehow he could totally relate.

Now that her friendship with Ally has recharged, Zee thought her sad song might have a happy ending, a hook that embodied hope and lifelong bonds, perhaps. *Duh de duh duh de duhhh,* she hummed. *Hmm... I know who would be great at helping me put this song together.*

Just then, after a week of no communication, she spotted Jasper Chapman across the quad talking casually to a passing student, looking quite pleased with whatever they were talking about. His smile was visible to Zee meters away, and like a magnet she started to jog his way, as if his smile had a strong pull on her body.

"Jasper! Hey," Zee said as she made eye contact with Jasper.

He looked at her surprised. "Oh hey, Zee, what's up?"

"Nothing, old pal," Zee said. "I haven't heard from you in, like, forever!"

"Yeah, I guess we missed each other before break," Jasper said. "Did you have a good one? Did you get to see any of London?"

"My mom and I went out for a few restaurants in Notting Hill, but I went to Paris in the middle of the week to see Ally."

"Ally! How is she doing?"

"She's okay, but her parents are splitting up, so that's been tough."

"Oh, sorry to hear that."

"I thought I would have heard from you over break so that you could show me some parts of London," Zee said.

Jasper shifted on his heels. "I guess I got caught up in family stuff. When I didn't see you before you left, I figured you were busy."

"Well, I'm around now, and I'm in the middle of working on my song for the Festival. I can really use your help. Can we get together for a music session, like old times in Brookdale?"

"Of course, any time," Jasper said.

"Would tomorrow afternoon work?"

"Yep, perfect. We'll meet after prep."

"Great! It'll be nice to catch up, just the two of us," Zee said.

Jasper started to back away toward the lecture hall where his first class was. The smile softened. "I'll see you tomorrow," Jasper said, and he trotted off to class.

Zee watched him leave, wondering if he was as excited about their musical reunion as she was.

···

In algebra class, Zee sat on the opposite side of the room from Jasper to avoid being even more distracted than usual during the lecture. But when Izzy walked into the classroom, she was recording her excited entrance for her latest YouTube video and couldn't help but draw attention. "Good morning, all! Are we ready for another Monday?" Izzy said, then pointed the camera directly at Zee. "Zee! How are you? We have to catch up in study group!" The students all waved and made faces, but everyone straightened up once Mr. Stevens walked into the room.

After greeting the class and introducing the day's lesson, Mr. Stevens rambled on about formulas and division. Zee took notes, thought about what she should eat for lunch, wondered if Archie was going to come back to music theory class today, worried that she forgot her favorite T-shirt back in her London bedroom, and debated in her mind whether or not Camilla had a boyfriend. The school bell rang before she could win the internal debate with herself and she went off to sciences.

At least in sciences, in which the theme of study changed every six weeks, the topic was now one that was of interest to her—the oceans. Before break, Mr. Roth had announced that the class would be studying the ecosystem of the oceans and the impact of pollution on its beings. After struggling through the last theme of the class on circuitry, Zee thought she could improve her grade since the new focus was one she liked. She bought a brand-new notebook for this section of sciences, eager for the change of topic.

Zee was awake for every word of Mr. Roth's lecture and

raised her hand to answer a few of the questions. *This is so my jam*, Zee thought. She looked over at Jasper and gave a wave and smile, and he raised his eyebrows as if to say, *Yay, oceans!* in the same weirdly encouraging manner that Zee might say to her twin baby siblings. Zee looked back at her books, eagerly took notes, and tried to shake the nagging feeling Jasper just wasn't into Zee's interests—like saving the oceans or being friends with Archie Saint John—as she was.

• • •

Zee sat in her English literature class wondering if the texts that the teachers picked for year nine were the same each year. How many year nine students had sat in her same seat, daydreaming about what flavor scones the dining hall might have today instead of focusing on the lecture? Yes, the speech written by yet another dead guy about freedom was important. Motivational, even. But interesting? Not so much.

In between listening to the lecture and taking notes, Zee's mind drifted off to her Festival performance. She visualized herself standing on the stage in front of the crowd. How big would that crowd be, she wondered. Did it include the whole school? Maybe some parents? All of the parents? And teachers and faculty? *That's huge!*

And she'd be up there with... Archie? No, he was going to perform his own song. Jasper? But he didn't really perform on stage because he arranged songs in the background. So she'd be alone? Zee was used to performing with her bandmates, and the Festival would be the first time she would perform alone to that large of a crowd. *Yikes. Maybe I should rethink my performance...*

"Miss Carmichael?" a voice from the front of the room called.

Zee's eyes darted upward. "Yes, Mrs. Pender?"

The teacher paused, peering at Zee carefully before continuing. "I wanted to know your thoughts on the speech before I hand out the homework assignment."

Zee cleared her throat and wiggled in her seat. "Um, ahem, I thought it was slightly dry, but effective. It evoked emotion as well as gave a call to action."

Mrs. Pender looked at Zee. She raised an eyebrow, then looked back toward the chalkboard. "And what's the name of the speechwriter we're talking about again?"

Zee looked down at her notes. She could not for the life of her remember the speechwriter's name. It was nowhere in her notes, not in the margins of her notebook, and not on the chalkboard on the opposite wall with the lecture notes.

"Um," Zee said. "I... um..."

Riiiing! The class bell rang, dismissing the class for the period. Zee exhaled a sigh of relief and picked up her backpack. "Your homework assignment is in the syllabus notes," Mrs. Pender said. "Read the next thirty pages in the textbook."

Zee slinked out the door quietly with the rest of her classmates. After Zee was out of sight, Mrs. Pender sat down at her desk to write something important in her notebook as the rest of the students filed out of the classroom.

• • •

Jasper and Zee agreed to meet in one of the formal music

studios with a sound booth and some electronics needed to mix a song from scratch. The secluded room would provide them privacy and good acoustics. Zee arrived early for their meeting, bringing her new journal filled with song lyrics that she wrote for the Festival. She didn't know if what she'd written so far was good enough. She wanted Jasper to like her work. She also wanted the entire student body not to boo her off the stage.

Zee took the long way to the recording room, from the back of the auditorium and across the stage. She had never seen the auditorium from this angle before. She started singing some

lyrics to herself, then walked up the few steps to the wide, oblong-shaped stage. Her sneakers softly walked across the wood flooring until she got to the middle of the platform, then she looked out at where the audience would sit. There were a lot of seats in the auditorium. How would she occupy such a large space with just her voice? Her palms became damp. She walked toward the stairway again and climbed down from the stage just as Jasper entered the room.

"Hello, hello!" Jasper said. "Getting comfortable on that ol' stage?"

Zee hurried to him. "Just checking out the view from here."

"Yeah, this is one of my favorite places to play. It feels like the O2 Arena!" Jasper joked. "Well, sorta. You know, standing on the stage with the lights off and all those people staring back at you. Come on, let's hit the recording studio and hear what you've got so far."

Zee and Jasper went down the backstairs to the lower level and opened the door to the recording studio. They took their seats behind the large mixer and opened up their notes. Zee started to sing a few lines from the song she'd written so far. Jasper looked at her when she finished.

"That sounds all right," Jasper said. "What did you have in mind in terms of music?"

"Something acoustic, like an acoustic guitar background. Simple. Very coffeehouse. More mature, you know? Archie actually came up with a melody that sounded wonderful, so I've been toying around with that."

"Archie," Jasper said flatly.

"Yes, your best friend Archie."

"Easy there," Jasper snipped. "What did it sound like?"

Zee pulled up a note from her phone where Archie wrote down the chords he had given Zee during one of their early jam sessions. Jasper clicked around his screens and approached a keyboard. He played the exact notes Archie played on the guitar.

"That sounds good!" Zee said excitedly.

"It sounds a bit flat to me," Jasper said. "Remember, this is the Festival. Hundreds of people on a Friday night. They want to be entertained, not lulled to sleep."

Zee was taken aback. Back in the delays of performing with The Beans, Jasper had never said anything negative about Zee's songs, even if they did need some work. The two usually collaborated together seamlessly to add a drumbeat or a cymbal or backing track to make it come together.

"You don't like it because it's flat, or because Archie wrote it?" Zee asked.

"I just think we can punch it up a bit more. Why don't we layer on, yeah?"

Jasper clicked through a bunch of screens and stored sound effects on his computer, searching for some backing music that could fill out Zee's song. He hummed to himself. Then he went on the Internet for a quick browse on some music sites and clicked on the website of some band he liked. "They've got a new album coming out," he said. Jasper was obsessed with music, but seemed to care less about Zee's music.

Zee looked at him. "Um, hi? Remember me? Remember my song?"

"Hmm? Yeah, right, I'm looking for melodies."

"Uh-huh," Zee said. They sat in silence while Jasper browsed and Zee stared at him browsing. Jasper didn't even ask who

Zee's song was about. He also didn't care to ask about her day, her break, or her sciences grade. Now that her biggest former cheerleader is nonplussed by her music, Zee was feeling even more insecure about her performance.

"Tell you what," Jasper said, "why don't I do some research on this for another day or two and send you some ideas? I work best when I can just jam out random notes and see what sticks. Sound good?"

Zee nodded. "So you think the song's good?"

"Yeah, it just needs fine-tuning. You'll be great. I'll e-mail you some stuff." Jasper gathered his notes and laptop into his backpack and grabbed his jacket. "We'll go back and forth until it's perfect, just like old times."

Zee looked and him and nodded. "Old, easy, fun times," she replied, and followed Jasper out of the recording studio.

5

SURPRISE VISIT

The first week back at The Hollows flew by. Algebra quizzes, science experiments, and a heavy amount of reading for both English lit and art history took up more of Zee's time than she wanted. Whatever spare time she had left she spent refining her song for the Festival. So on Saturday, Zee cleared her schedule for a marathon study and writing session where she could fully concentrate without being distracted by anyone or anything. Her only extracurricular activity would be to upload new photos to the Zee Files to share with Ally and Chloe, and to apply a face mask.

Just twenty minutes into her scheduled study session, the dorm advisor, Elizabeth, knocked on Zee's door. "Zee, you have a visitor. He's waiting downstairs."

Zee turned back toward her closet and grabbed her favorite cardigan, the black cashmere one she brought from home. She took a glance at herself in the mirror to make sure she didn't have any leftover face mask on her face, then opened the door. Zee wondered who was waiting for her. Archie? Did he bring her tea? Was this his way of saying that their jam sessions were becoming more than just jam sessions?

Zee followed the dorm advisor down the stairs, clearing her throat and nervously smoothing her hair behind her ear. Ahead of her, Elizabeth tapped someone on the shoulder. He was much taller than Archie, wider than Archie, and had lighter hair than Archie. Then he turned around and excitedly looked at Zee.

"Surprise!" Mr. Carmichael said as he stretched his arms toward his daughter. "I had a project in town so I thought I'd come see you."

"Dad! Hi!" Zee said, stunned. "On a Saturday?"

"It was the only time this photo shoot for work could happen. How are you, my dear? Did you just wake up?"

"No! I was just reading in bed. Slow morning. Hi!" Zee hugged him back.

"I thought we could go out for a late breakfast and catch up. Sound good?"

"Yeah!" Zee looked down at her pajama pants and oversized T-shirt. "Let me get changed."

"I'll wait here and answer some e-mails. Take your time. Oh, your mother wanted me to bring these. Extra socks and things you might need." Mr. Carmichael handed Zee a shopping bag.

Zee took the large bag and went back up the stairs, excited for the arrival of both a familiar face, a special gift, and a tasty breakfast. She was craving fried eggs with avocado. And maybe some grapefruit juice. *And after breakfast, maybe Dad can take me to the stationers and I can pick up a new journal?* Zee already forgot about her uninterrupted day of studying.

She returned to her room and opened the bag on her bed. Looking inside, she found six extra pairs of socks, a dozen extra pairs of underwear, and the softest silk scarf and handknit beanie she'd ever owned. Zee reached for a beautifully handwritten note addressed to Zee on stationery from the name of a French boutique they popped into right after they took photos in front of the Eiffel Tower.

Paris wasn't just all about shopping for myself, it read. *Thought you might like these. Love you, my dear. Mom.*

• • •

Zee and her father tucked into a corner booth at Beanies, the popular restaurant about twenty minutes away and a stone's throw from Soho Farmhouse, where her father's company was producing a shoot for an ad campaign. The sun warmed their seats and bounced off their cups of tea and place settings. The menu included exactly what Zee was craving—fried eggs with a side of avocado. Zee and her father placed their orders with their attentive server. Once the server left them alone, Mr. Carmichael leaned toward his daughter.

"So my dear, how is everything going?"

"It's busy," Zee said. "It's a good thing I had that break last week, because it's just go-go-go now."

"It's getting to the hectic bits, huh?" Mr. Carmichael said, looking into Zee's eyes.

"Yeah, I mean, school and the Festival, but I... I dunno."

"Yes, but the Festival is an extracurricular, in my opinion. What about your actual classes? Like algebra and your English lit class?"

Zee became nervous. Her dad's tone was that of a lawyer's cross-examining a witness in court. "Well, I'm trying hard to balance it all," Zee said.

Mr. Carmichael leaned back in his seat. His hand went to his jacket pocket and he pulled out what looked like a letter. Zee had no idea who had written it or what it said, but she had a feeling neither she nor her father would be very happy with the information the letter would reveal.

"I have to tell you that your teachers are concerned about your performance," Mr. Carmichael said. He started to unfold

the letter. "I received this from your English teacher, Mrs. Pender. She wrote to me after classes closed up for fall break. She said, 'Mackenzie is not as attentive as she could be in our class. She's also not receiving the best marks on quizzes or exams, though her essays are quite strong. I know she knows this material and I know she's quite strong in English given her creative background. But I fear her lack of focus will only lead to even poorer performance. I'd like to try to work with you both to prevent this from happening as soon as possible.'"

Zee's heart fell to her knees. She'd never received any disciplinary notes for action from any teacher in her entire school career. She'd never done anything to start trouble in class or had any sort of academic troubles besides a few subpar quizzes here or there, which she always made up for with extra credit or study time. Mrs. Pender's words stung like a hungry wasp. But Zee knew as harsh as those words were, they weren't inaccurate.

Her father's pursed lips and stern stare wore Zee down by the second. She felt her throat become tight and her teeth clenched in her mouth. "Um, well, I guess it has been harder than I thought," Zee started.

"I checked with a few of your other teachers and they have said similar things," said Mr. Carmichael. "Is the schoolwork too hard? Are you not studying enough?"

"I... I..." There was no talking around the reality that the move to London and the British academic system were much harder than Zee bargained for. Zee was overwhelmed at school and overcome with emotion. She started to cry at the lunch table over her eggs.

"Oh, honey," her father started, reaching his arm around

her shoulder, pulling her toward him.

"I just want to make everyone happy!" Zee blurted out. "That's what I do! I make you and Mom happy! I make my friends happy! And I just want to make friends and write good songs and look good on Izzy's YouTube channel and feel smart enough to talk to Jameela, and I can't seem to find the time. There's just no time! No time to be happy!" Zee, gasping for air, reached for a napkin to dab the tears from her eyes.

"Whoa, calm down," Mr. Carmichael said. "Start at the beginning. What do you mean there's no time? What do you do all day?"

Zee sniffed back tears. "I wake up at 7 a.m., I go straight to class, I study, I have study groups, then after class I work on music. There's not a moment where I'm just goofing off."

"Okay, I believe you," Mr. Carmichael replied. "Then what are you so nervous about? You're only a few weeks into the semester." Mr. Carmichael gave Zee's hand a gentle squeeze. "Look, your teachers say that you want to do well, but when it comes to the tests or quizzes you struggle. Your arts teachers were more complimentary, but they also said you space off at times."

"Yeah, but that's just me, you know. I'm a creative, like you."

"There's creative, and then there's attentive. And you still need to pay attention and perform in class, Zee."

"Yeah," Zee said, and picked at her eggs. She was struggling. And for Zee, struggle was failure. And failing made Zee feel like more of an outcast, since she was already the new kid at boarding school and now she would be the new kid who was failing at boarding school. Her father seemed so far away though he was just on the other side of the table. All of a sudden, everything felt very far away—Ally, Jasper, Chloe, her parents, Archie, even her food. It was as if she were all alone in this world.

Her father sat back in the booth. "Maybe you should talk to someone about how you're feeling."

Zee looked at him sharply. "I don't want anyone to know I'm struggling in school. That will make it all worse!"

"I mean talk to a counselor, or a therapist."

Zee looked out the window. How did things get this bad? She thought she had it under control. She made new friends. She was working on new music. She had Archie. And would Archie hang out with her if she was a hot mess? But she did leave behind her true friends, her real home, and her parents to come to London—which was not an easy feat.

Mr. Carmichael leaned toward her. "Look, I'm sorry. I thought boarding school would be great because you would be around kids going through the same things all the time and could find some solace there. But it's a big shift to leave the only home you've known for most of your life, move to a new country, and then leave your parents to go and live with strangers."

"Yeah, it is," Zee said, blowing her nose.

"A counselor would be a person you could talk to about it. You could explain what you're going through, maybe get some help and some ideas to help you manage the stress."

Zee took a deep breath. She looked at the letter Mrs. Pender wrote her father. She wondered if more notes from other teachers would follow.

"What if my friends find out?" Zee asked.

"They won't. What you tell a therapist is completely

confidential. We don't even have to tell your mother if you don't want her to know."

"Are you going to tell Mom?" Zee worried. "I don't want her to know. She'll be disappointed."

Her father looked at her. "No, she won't be disappointed. She'll be happy you're tackling your issues head on with a professional. But if you really don't want to tell Mom, we don't have to."

Zee's throat started to loosen. Her breathing returned to a regular rhythm. "I'm sorry I let you down."

"You didn't let me down! But you have to get some help so you can turn things around. So, let's see that therapist."

"Okay," Zee said. "Promise you won't tell Mom?"

Mr. Carmichael stuck his pinky out. "Only if you promise to have lunch with me more often, and that if you ever feel as stressed out as you did today, you call me."

Zee wiped her face and wrapped her pinky around her father's and pulled their hands down toward the floor. "Deal," she said.

6

SOMEONE TO TALK TO

*T*ucked into a corner office of the main administrative building of The Hollows, a tall woman with jet-black hair as shiny as a magazine cover and smooth brown skin sat behind a glass desk. In front of her was a laptop, a Smythson notebook, and a legal pad. A cell phone and a tape recorder lay on top of the legal pad. The woman, looking over her calendar for the day, pushed back the sleeve of the cream-colored blazer she wore with a silk blouse and a pair of slim-fit jeans. On the wall hung degrees from Stanford and Cambridge Universities with her name in bold letters: Dr. Emma Banks, Ph.D.

A knock on the office door grabbed Dr. Banks's attention, and she stood up from behind her desk, her patent leather heels adding another three inches in height. "Yes? It's open." Zee pushed the door open and slowly walked toward the school psychologist.

"Hi, Mackenzie? I'm Dr. Banks," the tall woman greeted, standing from behind the desk and reaching out her hand to shake Zee's.

"Hi, um, nice to meet you." Zee blinked a few times. "You're the therapist?"

"Yes. I've been here for the last five years. How are you doing?"

Zee slowly took a seat across from the desk. "Um, I'm okay. For now."

Dr. Banks nodded slowly. "Are you nervous? That's understandable. People hear the words 'counseling' and 'therapy' and think the worst, of themselves and of what therapy means. But this is a safe space. You can speak freely about anything, and whatever we talk about stays here in this room."

Zee clasped her hands together in her lap and wrung them nervously. She searched for something to say. "So, do I just start? How does this go? I mean, I've never done this before."

"No worries. How about I share a bit about myself so you don't feel like you're the only one doing all of the sharing?"

"Okay," said Zee.

"All right. Like I said, I've been a therapist here for five years. But I've been a psychologist for ten years, working with people about your age mostly. I'm here just to listen to what's going on in their lives and offer some tools and understanding of how to best manage whatever things they feel are unmanageable."

"Like algebra homework?"

"Yes," Dr. Banks said, chuckling. "Like school studies, or family situations, or any other sort of pressures or issues one your age might face."

"Uh-huh," Zee said. "How do you even know what a kid goes through? You, um, haven't been a kid in quite some time."

Dr. Banks smiled, her head leaning toward her right

shoulder. "Ha! Well, I was a kid not so long ago! Plus I have a family myself, so I can understand how important family relations can be."

"You do?"

"Yes, I have a son and a husband," Dr. Banks said.

"How old are they?"

"My husband is slightly younger than your dad. And my son is three. We live close by, in Cheshire."

"Oh," Zee said, imagining Dr. Banks's life outside of her office. Zee looked around and eyed the pictures on Dr. Banks's desk. In one, a smiling little brown boy sat on what she assumed to be Dr. Banks's husband's lap, while Dr. Banks stared back at them.

"So, Mackenzie..."

"You can call me Zee," Zee interrupted. "Everyone does."

"Ah, okay, Zee," Dr. Banks corrected herself. "What brings you here today?"

"My dad made me come?"

"Yes, I'm aware," Dr. Banks said, grabbing her legal pad. "But what is going on with you? Let's start by talking about what's going well right now. People always start with the problems, but I like to start with the fun things. If we talk about the good things, maybe we can figure out why other things don't feel so good."

Zee nodded. "Okay. Let's see. What's going well is music. I'm working on a song for the Festival."

"Ah, the Festival! That's always a great event around here. Is that your main hobby, music?"

"Yes," Zee said.

"Do you sing or play an instrument?"

"I mainly sing and write songs. And I play guitar. I was part of a band back in California called The Beans. We were popular at our school. Performed at assemblies and events. We even performed on television a few times."

"Cool," Dr. Banks replied. "So you must be excited for the Festival coming up?"

"I was," Zee sighed. "The one happy point in my life had been the Festival, but now I'm nervous about doing it. My roommate, Jameela, makes it sounds like it's an audition for American Idol. I mean, I thought it was a showcase of creative expression and who I am as a person. But it seems rather competitive."

"I see," said Dr. Banks. "Does that make you frustrated?"

"It does kind of take the joy out of it, thinking that I'm auditioning for some big break," Zee said. She rested her elbows on her knees and her head in the palms of her hands.

"I recall the Festival being more relaxed, but students take their performances very seriously."

Zee felt words start to rise up into her throat, as if they wanted to rush out of her body like a roaring river. "It's just yet another example of this pressure to be together and perfect all the time. Like, my old school is more about expressing your ideas and being creative and unique and free spirited, and not being afraid to fail. But here, things seem much more rigid."

"Well, there are no judges at the Festival, and the faculty encourages students to perform whatever does represent them creatively. What kind of song are you writing for it?"

Zee thought about how best to describe her half-formed song about relationships in her life. "It's a thoughtful ballad."

"Ah, so you'll sing alone?"

"I guess. It would be my first time performing solo in a long time. I usually perform with friends. My friend Archie gave me a backing melody for the song, and my other friend Jasper will arrange it for me. So, I dunno."

"That's lovely. Have you known them a long time?"

"I've known Jasper a while because he went to my school in California for a bit. That's why I ended up here, because his parents told my parents about the school and my parents signed me up."

"Right. And how do you know Archie?"

Zee spoke carefully about her history with Archie. "I met Archie here. He's a new friend. He's... interesting."

"That all sounds great," Dr. Banks said, scribbling notes on her legal pad and nodding her head. "So it sounds to me while you're frustrated about the pressure of performing, and the process of creating your music is going well. And you have some friends you're working with on the music."

"Yeah, that's right."

"Okay," Dr. Banks said. "So now tell me what you're nervous about. What seems to be the things that aren't going as you expected?"

Zee shifted in her seat, wringing her sweaty palms. Her eyes darted around the room as she spoke. "Um, well, the schoolwork here is more challenging than it was back in California. And I want to do well, but everyone just seems to know more than I do."

"I see," Dr. Banks said. "Why do you think they know more than you do? Because they've gone to school here for a longer period of time?"

"Yeah, maybe that's it? I don't know." Zee said. She looked out the window behind Dr. Banks's desk. "They're also, like, well traveled."

"You're well traveled too. You're the only one from this school from California. I checked our school records."

"Yeah, but I'm new to the boarding school thing. And it's very different from regular school. I've never spent so much time away from home. I like my house. I like sleeping at my house. I'm not good at sleeping in a strange bed. And everyone acts like it's not a big deal here."

"I see," Dr. Banks said, still scribbling on her legal pad. "Tell me about your roommate. Do you two get on well?"

"Other than the fact that she can be super serious sometimes, yes. She's very into the rules and the proper way of doing things. And being the best."

"Right. Do you have other girlfriends on campus?"

"I met Izzy Matthews in the dorm."

"Izzy Matthews. Yes, I've heard of her," Dr. Banks said, looking up from her legal pad. "So you've made some friends, you're performing at the Festival, but you're nervous about your performance and being new at school, is that what I'm hearing?"

"I guess."

"Okay. All right. So now, I want you to think about the positive aspects of all those things. What's going well with the song? What's going well with your friends? Is there any particular friend who's been lovely to you or done something to support you? And with your roommate, is there something she's done to help you or make you feel good?"

Zee thought about her last jam session with Archie—he effortlessly put together breezy guitar chords for her lyrics which helped shape her song. She thought about how Jasper brought her those extra study notes for her circuitry class to help her get a better grade on the last exam. It was the best grade she got all term so far. And then she thought about that awesome weekend at Izzy's estate, where they swam and ate yummy food and laughed at silly jokes during the sleepover. Then she thought about the other night when Jameela showed her how to meditate. Zee looked at the ceiling and nodded slowly. *Maybe things aren't so bad*, she thought.

"For the next few days, try to remember the good parts of these more challenging situations. Focus on one or two of the good things about school. Let's end this session on a positive note thinking about the good stuff. And the next time we meet, we can dive into some specific issues you're having. That sound all right?"

Zee felt relieved. "Yeah, sounds good."

"Great, I'll see you next week," Dr. Banks said, standing up from her seat and reaching out to shake Zee's hand. Zee returned the gesture, smiling, feeling a bit lighter in the chest as she walked out toward the building exit.

7

PRESSURE TO PERFORM

Girls, you won't believe what I just did, Zee wrote to Ally and Chloe in the Zee Files after class. Zee was reluctant to let anyone know she was in therapy, but she needed to tell her best friends not only was she in therapy, but that her therapist was beautiful and kind and wore high heels and looked like she would totally have been their band manager had they still been together playing as The Beans. Zee searched the Internet for a GIF that could visually explain where she was this afternoon. She found a short loop video of a cat sitting on a chaise lounge with its arms resting on its belly. Another cat wearing glasses sat in a chair with a clipboard. Zee posted the photo with the caption: *I went to therapy.*

Zee closed the computer, not expecting to hear from either one of them for many hours since it was early in the morning in California and just after school let out in Paris. But a few minutes later, Chloe called Zee directly. "Zee! What's wrong? Are you okay?"

"Hiiiiii," Zee replied. "I'm fine. My English lit teacher

wrote a note home saying I'm struggling in class. Dad made me go talk to someone."

"But you have us! Could you not talk to us?"

"Yeah," Zee explained. "But I need to talk to someone who's paid to listen to other people's problems. You all are busy with your own stuff."

"Still, Zee, you know we're always here for you. What's been bothering you?"

"I dunno. Moving and school, I guess..."

"But you said that things were going okay."

"Uh, since when is failing science pop quizzes okay?"

"When did that happen?" Chloe asked. "But you've got music and your new friends. And you've got Izzy and Archie and Jasper, right?"

"What I have is my teachers writing notes to my parents telling them I'm distracted and flighty in class. I've got an upset father who showed up at my dorm unannounced to tell me my teachers have warned him about my schoolwork. And now I have a weekly appointment with a therapist so she can listen to me complain and help me pass year nine."

"So, what's she like?" Chloe asked.

"Who, the therapist?" asked Zee. "Like a model. She's almost too pretty to understand my problems."

"Model therapist? That's intimidating."

"Yeah, but she's, like, super nice. And I told her, like, everything."

"Well, like you said, it's her job to listen," Chloe said.

"Yeah."

"Can you send us a photo?"

Zee did a quick Google search for Dr. Banks. The first

item that popped up was a listing for something called the International Directory of Psychologists and Therapists, which had a short profile and headshot of her. Zee copied and pasted the headshot and sent it to the girls.

"She's definitely pretty. Does she know about Archie? About your thing with him?" Chloe asked.

"No," said Zee. "That's the stuff I save for you guys."

Zee heard running water on the other end of the phone. Chloe was brushing her teeth and trying to talk at the same time. "Mmpfjioyk, I gwrotta gwret wready for scshoooll, but I whranted to cszheck in on shyooo. *Pyyyt-too! Ack!* Let me know if you're stressed out and need to chat. I'm always here."

"Thanks, I'll be fine."

"Okay, let's chat soon," Chloe said. "Love you!"

· · ·

Just as Zee hung up with Chloe, a text came in from her dad. *How did it go?*

Zee took a deep breath before replying.

Zee

> Fine. No need to call the
> paramedics just yet.

Dad

> I didn't think that would be
> necessary. So how many times
> a week will you see her?

> We worked out once a week. That okay?

Dad

> Perfect. Keep me posted on how things go.

Dad

> And no, I won't tell your mother.

• • •

It had been a few days since Zee, Tom, Jameela, and Jasper could all meet at the same time for dinner together between practices for Festival performances, sport, study groups, and other meetings. So when dinner finally synced for the group, Zee felt relief, eager to catch up in the main dining hall cafeteria.

Zee saw Jameela in the food court, eyeing the salads, and called out to her as she darted for the daily specials. Tom was already at their usual table, and Zee and Jameela joined him as he dog-eared a page in his English lit textbook and looked up. Jasper slid into the chair next to him with a chicken pot pie and lemonade on his tray.

"So, how's everyone's Festival performances going?" Jameela asked coolly.

"All right, I suppose," Zee said.

"Are you still working on that song?" Jameela asked. "I haven't heard so much as a note so far."

"Well, I'm still working out the lyrics."

"And I'm still working on the arrangement," Jasper chimed in.

"A duet!" Jameela said. "That should be fun on stage."

"Oh no, I'm more of a behind-the-scenes guy," Jasper answered. "Zee will be performing a solo."

"I see. Zee, all by yourself on stage. That should be amazing. And intense," Jameela said.

"You're performing solo for your ballet performance," Zee said. "Also intense."

"True, but since I'm dancing and moving around the stage I feel like it'll be easier to command the audience's attention. When you're singing a solo, you're just standing there on stage by yourself. It's all on you and your voice."

Zee felt that nervous twinge again, followed by that familiar fire rising into her throat once again. "Thanks for the words of encouragement, Jameela," she said.

"Tom, how's everything going with your spoken word jam?"

"Moving along smoothly, as usual," he said, smiling. "I'm experimenting with a few different approaches."

"Approaches?" Zee asked.

"Yeah, I'm debating whether I should include a drum or bongos, or just, like, recite it spoken word style. I also don't know how fast or how slow I'll spit my rhymes. I'm still working on it."

"Fabulous," Jameela said. "Anybody know what other performances are going on?"

Tom was halfway through his sandwich but put it back down on his plate. "I heard that one of the year ten students is doing some sort of drum percussion–type of set. That'll get the crowd hype."

"Yeah, and I hear another one is doing some sort of tribal African dance thing," Jasper added.

Jameela nodded. "Remember last year that guy who did the DJ set with the lightshow? And basically a big rave broke out during the Festival, and even the headmaster was jamming out to it?"

"Grant Morland. He was pretty great," Tom said. "The crowd holding their cell phones in the air gave it all a real Tomorrowland vibe."

"And that was after Penelope Drithers did that one-woman interactive theater piece that basically put everyone to sleep. Then everyone woke up once Grant's drum and bass kicked on," Jameela said.

"Yeah, but don't knock Penelope," Jasper said. "I heard the Cambridge Theatre offered her an audition, and this winter she's performing in *Matilda* there."

"What? That's amazing," Jameela said. "See, Zee, I told you your big break could come from a solid Festival performance."

Zee's eyes darted around the table. Lightshow? One-woman theater sketch? These kids were putting together the type of performances that won awards, not just impressed their fellow peers. But maybe Jameela was right: maybe the Festival was a jumping-off point to stardom, and maybe it was considered so because the students were extraordinarily talented. Zee started to worry about her own performance. What if it wasn't captivating enough? What if it was—just as Jasper described the other day—flat?

8

DEAR DIARY

ost classrooms at The Hollows were designed for interaction, with students sitting in pairs at tables or stations versus individual desks. Algebra was one of the few classes where students sat alone. Mr. Stevens allowed his students to choose whatever seat they wanted each day, and Zee usually sat in the same front row seat close to the door, where she could peer into the hallway and look at people walking by.

Mr. Stevens gave a rapid-paced class lecture for forty-five minutes, throwing out as many examples of equations as possible to teach each theory. Zee took copious notes, but after twenty minutes she found herself gazing out the front door, noticing every little squeak of a shoe or cough as someone walked. Then her eyes honed in on the cracked linoleum of the hallway floor. She wondered how many feet had stepped across that line. How many books were in all of the lockers lining the walls? How many bricks were laid to construct the walls of the building?

Why did Mr. Stevens's voice sound so close?

"Miss Carmichael?"

Zee's thoughts jolted back to the classroom. "Yes, sir."

"Care to answer question fifteen for us?"

Zee looked down at the textbook, which she wasn't even sure was open to the right chapter, let alone the right page.

"I've written it on the board for your convenience," Mr. Stevens said, pointing with a piece of chalk to the formula in white block letters on the chalkboard.

Zee studied the formula, chewing her upper lip as she did the calculation in her head. "Three. X is three," she said, confidently.

"And what's Y?" Mr. Stevens asked.

Dang it, I haven't escaped yet! Zee thought. "Um, Y is..." Zee blinked hard. "Two."

"Hmm," Mr. Stevens said, slowly walking toward Zee. Her heart started racing as he moved closer. *Am I right? Wrong? Why is he keeping me in suspense? If I'm wrong, then put me out of my misery and ask someone who knows!*

"Nice work, Miss Carmichael," Mr. Stevens said. "All right, let's move on."

Zee unclenched her teeth and let her muscles relax in her legs. *Why does the mere proximity of Mr. Stevens make me freak out?* Zee wondered. *I studied the lesson, I knew the answer. Why worry?*

Zee drummed her pencil against her algebra textbook, her eyes looking over the numbers in each formula until they turned blurry. When they did, she looked back out toward the exit, wondering how many invisible steps it would take her to slip out of class and underneath the safe covers of her bed.

• • •

Dr. Banks looked at Zee as she sat in the chair, twiddling her thumbs. Zee stared at how one thumb disappeared under the other, then noticed her nails, her chewed-on hangnails and the small ridges on the top of one nail. *I need to put hand lotion on my school shopping list, stat,* she thought. *And some glitter nail polish.*

"So, what's going on this week?" Dr. Banks asked. "How are you feeling?"

Zee shrugged and looked above Dr. Banks's head. "Nervous still."

"How are your classes?"

"Good. Well, some of them are good."

"Which ones?"

"Art. Music. Skills for Life. Most of the ones where I get to do something in class besides take notes."

"Ah, gotcha." Dr. Banks wrote something down on her legal pad. "So, algebra class. Tell me about that. That's with Mr. Stevens, yes?"

"Yes. Not my favorite subject."

"How do you feel in the class?"

"Like I want to leave."

"Any particular reason why? Do you not understand the work? Is your teacher intimidating?"

"No, I understand most of it."

"Where do you sit in class? Toward the front or back?"

"I sit by the door. Usually no one sits behind me."

"Right. And that class has individual desks, right? You sit in a single seat?"

"Yes."

"Not as fun as sitting with a partner, I imagine."

"Nope.

"Actually, kinda lonely, right?"

Zee thought about it. "Maybe. Definitely makes it more intimidating when teachers call on you."

"You've mentioned feeling out of place or all alone before, when you talked about your move here to London and going to boarding school for the first time. Do you think maybe sitting alone stirs up those feelings of being alone again?"

"Hmm." Zee shrugged her shoulders. "Maybe?"

"Do you get nervous being called out to answer questions in class?"

"Yes."

"What are you scared of?"

Zee tapped her foot on the floor nervously. "Could be I just don't want to be wrong."

"I see. That's understandable. No one wants to be embarrassed."

Dr. Banks put down her legal pad and went over to her laptop. She took a minute or two to look for a document, then printed it out on her printer. She came back to the seat in front of Zee and leaned in closely, showing the paper to Zee.

"Let's try a different exercise this week," Dr. Banks said. "Since you're a writer and writing is your strong suit, let's try a journaling exercise. This is called target journaling, where you can pick from one of the prompts here and use that to start a journal entry."

Zee took the paper and looked it over. It included thirty open-ended questions about everything from childhood memories to favorite foods to annoying sounds.

"The great thing is you can do them in any order you like, whenever you like. And you don't have to show me if you don't want to. The idea is to use your time while journaling to reflect but also tap into other times in your life when you have felt certain emotions, and use those memories to help you through what you're dealing with now," Dr. Banks said.

Zee nodded her head. "Okay."

"Great. Don't worry, I don't have to read your work. And don't worry about editing or sounding perfect. Just write freely and from the heart."

Finally, homework that doesn't have to be perfect, Zee thought. It was the first homework assignment at The Hollows Zee knew she would ace.

• • •

Zee came back to her room for a short break between music theory and prep. The room was quiet—Jameela was out at ballet practice and her bed was made and her desk tidy. Zee's bed comforter was folded back, left in the same position after she got up this morning. Her schoolbooks were strewn on the floor next to her nightstand. She dumped her backpack near her desk. A dirty sock had missed the hamper and lay on the floor nearby, and a few worn uniform shirts hung over the desk chair.

Zee flopped down on the bed and sighed. Her body relaxed into the bedding. She turned her head over to one side and saw her journal.

She sat up in her bed and remembered Dr. Banks's

assignment. She looked at her backpack where she'd stuffed the targeted journaling worksheet and dug it out of the front pocket. Then she unfolded it and looked over the questions again. Leaning back on her pillow, she grabbed her journal and her favorite black gel pen, and started writing.

The first question on the worksheet read: *When in your life was the happiest time of your life?*

Zee looked up at the ceiling, scanning her thoughts for good memories of her first dozen or so years on earth. She settled on a moment and let her pen hit the paper.

Life was amazing back in Brookdale. My friends lived around the corner. My family and I hung out all the time and we did almost everything together. My best friends and I were in a band, The Beans, and we were very popular in town—we even got to play on television. My school was awesome. We recycled and composted and did so many fun projects to save the planet. I skied in Lake Tahoe and surfed in San Diego. I roller skated in my front yard. I saw a ton of rainbows and birds and butterflies. And everything just seemed to be so easy then. The weather was even easy. It never rained or snowed. I hardly ever had a bad hair day.

The second question on the worksheet read: *When were you the saddest?*

Zee searched her memories again, and then she remembered the exact day. *The day my mom told us we would be moving to London.*

Zee looked at the words written down on the page. She remembered back to the day her dad told her they would be moving away. Chloe and Zee had already outlined their plans for eighth grade, which included both of them trying out for the traveling soccer team, Zee writing songs for The Beans, and Chloe editing the school paper. They were going to have a schedule where twice a week they would meet at each other's houses for study sessions and on the weekends for jam sessions. But their plans were derailed when Mr. Carmichael had come home and said, "Zee, my dear, we're going to London."

Zee remembered herself freezing at the word. "London?"

"Yes, London. We have an opportunity to move and send you to a fabulous school and experience a new country and culture. And we're moving at the end of summer."

"WHHHAAATTTTT?" Zee had said to her parents. She didn't think she'd do well with the change. But her parents figured Zee would adapt to the changes, just like the rest of the family would. "She'll be fine once we get there," Zee overheard Mr. Carmichael assure Mrs. Carmichael. Zee wondered though if even he, too, really believed if that would really be true.

Zee remembered that heart-stomping feeling of realizing she was going to leave behind everything she's known her whole life. Her school, her friends, her bedroom, her favorite stores, tacos, ice cream, her favorite everything. She remembered crying into her pillow for an hour that day, wondering if she'd ever remember California—or if California would ever remember her.

She closed the journal and curled up on her bed. Clutching one of her pillows tightly around her face, she released a loud "EEEEEEEEEEEEKKKK!" as that familiar fire rose up inside her ever since she arrived in London.

9

WORKING TOGETHER

Skills for Life was the one class that Zee didn't get distracted in. Perhaps it was because students were graded on a pass-or-fail scale, or because this quarter they were focused on cooking, and she and Tom were paired together to be partners and do the work together. Since both of them enjoyed foods like sprouts and chia seeds and kale, they cooked and ate well together. Izzy, Jasper, and Jameela were all paired with other students for the class. Izzy often covertly filmed during cooking lectures for her YouTube channel. Mrs. Templeton usually didn't allow Izzy to film during class, but she agreed to let Izzy film the class's upcoming final project, a hearty Sunday roast where every student had to bring a dish.

Tom and Zee sat together listening to Mrs. Templeton describe the various ways to cook eggs: scrambled, hard-boiled, poached, sunny-side up. Each pair of students would make eggs a different way, prepping their eggs at their stations first then bringing them to the hot ranges at the front of the classroom to cook them with Mrs. Templeton's assistance.

Mrs. Templeton assigned Tom and Zee to make theirs into an omelet.

Tom poked Zee on the shoulder. "I reckon you're a sunny-side up egg," he said jokingly.

"Aww, thanks, Tom," Zee said. "Though I haven't been feeling all that sunny lately."

"What's up?"

"I dunno," Zee said. "Just, like, stress. And I'm not making much progress on my Festival song."

"Really?" Tom said. "You know, eggs do have relaxing properties."

"They do?"

"Yeah, they say eggs are good for balance and making you feel more steady. They're packed with vitamins."

Zee smiled. "Right. Guess I should eat our assignment so I'll feel better?"

"Could help!"

Mrs. Templeton instructed the class to start prepping their eggs to cook. Zee cracked three eggs into a bowl. Tom added salt and pepper and began to stir.

"Do you practice yoga?" Tom asked Zee.

"I've done it a few times, but I don't, like, *practice*."

"Maybe try it. It's done wonders for me. From there, I got into meditation too. Which is truly a game changer."

"But you seem so calm all the time, you don't need yoga," Zee said.

"I'm calm because I *do* yoga," Tom said. "I used to be off my rocker when I was younger. We moved around so much that I could never get settled. But once I started doing yoga with my mum, I felt a lot calmer."

"It seems so hard though, to sit in one place with your eyes closed and not move. Jameela shared one of her meditation apps with me, and I fell asleep after a minute," Zee said.

"That's not the only way to meditate," Tom said. "You can do it by singing, or by visualization, like looking at a candle or an object. There are options."

"Really? I like singing."

Tom passed the bowl of eggs to Zee. She grabbed the whisk and started stirring.

"Why not start with something like a simple affirmation? Basically repeating a mantra on how you want to feel? Like 'I am peace' or 'I am love,'" he suggested.

"Can I say, 'I am a genius'?"

Tom chuckled. "If that is going to bring you harmony with your mind and body, sure. Repeat it for about a minute to start out. Then once you get the hang of it, try two minutes. Then three."

Zee considered this. "What do you say when you meditate?"

"I have a bunch of mantras I know from yoga or meditation books I've read. Depends on how I want to feel. But concentrate on breathing in and out through the nose, nice and steady, and relaxing your body. What you say will come after you do those things."

Mrs. Templeton approached their station. "All right, you two. Ready to cook?"

Zee and Tom followed Mrs. Templeton to one of the cook stations. "Okay, your eggs are mixed well, great. Did you season them?" Mrs. Templeton asked.

"Yes, ma'am," Tom said.

"All right. You can add some cheese from here, if you want." Mrs. Templeton gestured, and Tom grabbed a small bit of shredded cheddar cheese and tossed it into the bowl. Then he poured the egg mixture into a nonstick pan.

"Now, you let the eggs set about a minute or two on the one side—very nice. And then you work one side over the other," Mrs. Templeton said. Tom gently worked a spatula under the omelet and folded one half over the other. "Nice. Have you done this before?" she asked him.

"Yeah, a few times," Tom replied. "I watch a lot of Gordon Ramsay videos online."

"One way to learn to cook, I suppose," Mrs. Templeton said.

"Right, now we gently tip the pan toward us and let the omelet slide onto the plate." Tom followed her directions, and the omelet smoothly landed on the white serving plate.

"Great," Mrs. Templeton said. "And you can add a bit of garnish if you like, maybe some parsley if that tickles your fancy." Zee took a dash of chopped herbs in between her fingers and sprinkled it over the eggs. "Voila!"

Zee looked at the omelet and felt a sense of accomplishment, like an artist feeling a sense of satisfaction from making something beautiful out of nothing. Looking at the eggs, Zee saw a beautiful, nourishing plate of food made out of random refrigerator items. She was proud of her efforts. She took a bite, and felt even more satisfied. "Mmm, yummy," she said.

Tom ate some too. "Proper eggs right there."

Mrs. Templeton tasted their eggs, and nodded. "Nice work, you two. Perhaps you can come over to my place on Sunday and make brunch for me," she joked.

Zee smiled, taking another bite of her class assignment. "I'll bring the scones and tea."

• • •

Zee and Ally have still not spoken much since their Paris trip. For all the talk about keeping in touch she'd done, Ally left messages barely longer than a sentence or two in the Zee Files and rarely responded to a text in a timely fashion. Since Zee revealed to the girls she was in therapy, Ally's only response to the whole thing was about Dr. Banks: *She went to Stanford for grad school. Impressive.*

Zee texted Ally as she was leaving her last class of the day.

> **Hiiiii! How's everything in Paris?**

Zee kept her phone in her hand, waiting for a potential reply from Ally to come through. She looked out at the quad, then checked her calendar for the day. Study group with Jasper and Izzy was in fifteen minutes. Zee slowly walked toward the quad, looking down at her phone, waiting for Ally's reply. It never came.

"C'mon, Ally!" Zee grumbled at her phone, trying to will a text to come through from her BFF.

Just then, a familiar voice called to her. "You mean Archie, right? I'm right here, Cali!"

Zee looked as if she'd been caught with her hand in the cookie jar. As she looked up from her cell phone, Archie, in his Hollows uniform with a broad smile, was staring right at her. "Archie! What... where did you come from?"

"Thin air," he said. "Where have you been?"

"Um, around," Zee said, trying to mask surprise.

"Yeah, I know you've been around. I saw you coming out of Dr. Banks's office the other day."

Zee's stomach dropped. She didn't want anyone to know she was in therapy, much less Archie. "Um, I was just picking up something."

"Yeah, right. Anyway, how's that song coming? I haven't heard an update in a while."

"Oh, yeah, well, not much to update you on. Jasper is helping me arrange it."

"Jasper Chapman, eh? He's a good chap."

Zee looked puzzled. Jasper hasn't said a nice thing about Archie since she arrived. Archie seemed to be fonder of Jasper than Jasper was of him.

"So you got time for a catch-up with your ol' pal, me? Much to discuss, it seems," Archie said.

"Sure, but right now I'm heading to study group," Zee said.

"Ah, right. Tomorrow?"

"I'll text you," Zee said, walking toward the main library. She turned her head quickly, hoping Archie couldn't see her wincing from embarrassment of him knowing she was going to therapy as she walked on.

• • •

Izzy and Poppy had gathered at their usual study spot in the large study hall, their science and algebra textbooks already scattered on the table. Jasper arrived just as Izzy was filling in Poppy on her Festival project.

"So get this—the headmaster and the Festival director, Mr. Hysworth, asked me to take portraits of all our mates for a special photo exhibit they want at the school. It's going to be unveiled at the Festival and eventually live on campus permanently. How awesome is that?"

"That's great, Izzy!" Poppy replied. "And while you work on it, we can get some amazing BTS content for the vlog!"

"Exactly! I can shoot whoever I want, so long as I get an interesting mix of students from the entire school. And I can photograph them anywhere! I mean, obviously I'll include you guys," Izzy said.

Jasper looked at Izzy. "Make sure to get my good side."

"Which is both sides, right?" Izzy said, smiling.

"Ah, no, it's just my backside." Jasper turned his head 180 degrees so the back of his head faced the girls.

"Ha ha," Izzy said. "Because you're so eager to participate, why don't you come to my house for your photo shoot next weekend, silly?"

Jasper shrugged his shoulders. "All right. Let me know when. Your dad will pick us up?"

"Yep. We can leave Saturday morning and come back that evening. Super easy and professional."

"That's my nickname, Jasper Super Easy and Professional Chapman," he joked.

"You're cracking today!" Izzy said. "Let's get cracking on this algebra homework."

Zee came into the study hall just as they all opened their books. "Hey hey! Just what I wanted to see, formulas and friends."

"Right, today's lesson was killer, yeah?" Jasper said. He volunteered his own notes and went over the last few problems with the girls. Zee worked through a few of them on her own, then the group went silent as they read the next chapter's lesson.

An hour went by, and Zee felt like she had actually retained the information she studied. There were very few interruptions for vlogging or jokes, and Jasper and Izzy talked solely about their schoolwork. It was the most focused study group they'd had in weeks, and Zee felt content about the work they'd gotten done.

"Oh, I have to head out," Izzy said, looking at her phone. "I have club soccer today. Pops, you coming? Jasper, let me know about this weekend."

"Yep," he said quietly. Izzy and Poppy grabbed their books and headed out.

What's going on this weekend? Zee thought.

Jasper looked at his phone for the time. "I should get back to the dorm. I've got some music stuff to work on, including your song. Did you make any more changes to it?"

Zee closed her book slowly. "Not yet. Should we work on it together later this week?"

"Possibly," Jasper said, walking away from the table already. "Let me know when you're ready."

Zee barely got to wave goodbye before he left. As the last to leave the table, she gathered her notes together by herself and thought about how she didn't have time to ask Jasper and Izzy what in fact was going on this weekend. Whatever it was, Zee had a sinking feeling she wasn't invited.

10

MODEL STUDENT

*Z*ee came back to her dorm room, ready to exhale everything out from the day and change out of her uniform, which by now felt tight and constricting. Her favorite pajamas were freshly laundered and folded in the loads of clothes that had been cleaned by the on-campus cleaners. She pulled them from the tightly packed stack of clothes. "Mmm... smells like baby powder," she said, smoothing the fabric against her cheek.

After a quick shower and getting ready for bed, Zee checked her computer to see if Chloe and Ally left any news in the Zee Files. Chloe had uploaded a few photos of various braided hairstyles. *Which one should I get for the soccer sectionals next week?* she wrote in the captions. *We play four games over the weekend and I won't have time to think about hair.*

Zee flagged a few photos she liked, then looked for some activity from Ally. There was nothing.

Zee settled back into her bed, pulling the covers up to her waist. She reached for her phone and checked for any unread text messages, then pulled out her journal and wrote down song lyrics, feeling a tug at her heart after not hearing from Ally once again:

Waiting, wondering, fading from your eye
Hard to catch you, no matter how hard I try
Never meant to hurt you,
Even when you ran into
The abyss of you

Zee hummed the guitar riff Archie had played for her when she sang the opening chords for him. *I need Jasper's help with this, big time,* she thought. Zee grabbed her cell phone and send him a text.

Zee

> **SOS song help. You around tomorrow?**

A half hour later, Jasper replied.

Jasper

> **Can't tomorrow. Let's chat Monday.**

He's tied up the whole weekend? Zee thought.

She looked at the second line of her song: *Hard to catch you, no matter how hard I try.* Exactly, she thought, rereading Jasper's text, then shut off her phone.

• • •

On Saturday, Jasper and Izzy got picked up by her dad early in the morning. The ride to Izzy's family's home in Gloucestershire was a half hour from campus, and Izzy talked—and filmed—the entire way. She gave live commentary to her YouTube followers, then pointed the camera at Jasper. He tried to look out the window to avoid the camera, but Izzy got him to at least smile and flash a peace sign toward her.

"So what's your Festival piece about exactly?" Jasper asked when she put the camera down.

"I told you I was doing portraits of our schoolmates, black-and-whites oversized, right?"

"Yeah, but I didn't know who exactly you were shooting."

Izzy leaned in closely to him. "Well, you, for one. Today is your photo shoot day!"

"I'm aware," Jasper said flatly. "Do I look all right? Are you photographing everyone in uniform?"

"Yes, but you can rock accessories or style yourself any way you like. Jacket, no jacket, tie, no tie. Whatever. You look great."

Jasper felt butterflies in his stomach. He liked to stay behind the scenes, which is why he loved producing songs and music tracks for others. But since being in front of the camera would help his fellow friend produce something great, he agreed to grin and bear the attention to help Izzy shine.

"Don't worry, you're like the tenth subject Izzy's photographed for this project," said Izzy's dad, who looked at Jasper's nervous face in the rearview mirror. "It'll be fine. She's an old pro by now."

"We're here!" Izzy said as she hopped out the car. The family's English Spaniels, Kingston and Baron, ran up to the car, panting and wagging their tails. "The welcome committee," Izzy said, then led Jasper out.

Izzy took him by the hand toward the back of the house, where her staff had already set up her camera equipment for her photo sessions and a small snack bar on the right side of the patio. Izzy set up another camera on a tripod to take behind-the-scenes footage of herself shooting Jasper for her YouTube channel.

"All right, all you have to do is mill about and act natural," Izzy said.

"So easy for you to say, famous YouTube vlogger," Jasper joked.

"I'm serious. Sit tight, let me get a headshot of you."

Izzy moved in closely with her camera and snapped away. Jasper shyly moved his head to one side smiling while looking down at the ground. Izzy stood behind the camera, intensely focused on her work, the camera shutter repeatedly clicking.

"Great, now turn back and look the other way," Izzy said. Jasper did as he was told.

"Now jump with both arms in the air," Izzy said. Jasper bent his knees and took a leap upwards, laughing.

"I'm hardly a model," he said.

"You're modeling now," Izzy said, snapping away.

After a few minutes of candid shots, Izzy put the camera down. "Okay, now I'm going to ask you some questions, and you just keep acting naturally while I take photos."

"All right," Jasper said.

"What's your favorite food?"

"Um, tacos?"

"What's your favorite school subject?"

"Computer science."

"Right. What's your favorite part about London?"

Jasper took a beat to think. "The countryside."

Izzy looked at him. "What do you want to be when you grow up?"

"A famous music producer."

Izzy looked intently at him. "Have you ever been in love?"

Jasper paused. He knew the truth, but wasn't sure that was what Izzy wanted to hear. "Maybe," he teased.

Izzy's faced perked up. "Really? You'd know if you were."

"How would I know?"

"You'd know," Izzy replied, picking up her camera and snapping Jasper's surprised face.

After another ten minutes of questions, Izzy announced, "That's a wrap!" in dramatic form. Jasper, relieved for the shoot to be over, grabbed some crackers and cheese from the snacks on hand on the patio. "Let me show you around," Izzy said, then took him for a tour around her home.

Izzy showed him her portraits of friends and family members at vacations and events that her parents proudly displayed in the den. "I took this one of our family at the beach in Bali," she said. "Oh, and this one was skiing in Switzerland."

"Wow," Jasper said. "These are fantastic! Your pictures are seriously great."

"Thanks," Izzy said. "I wish I could do more of this during school."

"Why, because you're more focused on your YouTube channel?"

"Yeah, and it takes up so much time," Izzy said. "I love doing my vlog, but it's a ton of work. Some days I'm not sure it's worth it."

"Really?" Jasper asked, raising his eyebrows.

"Don't get me wrong. I like attention and clicks and the free stuff sometimes. But when your life is public, you're a public figure. And people feel like they know you. So then there are these people commenting on me and my life like they know me. And they only know what I choose to put on the channel. Do people know I ski? Nope, because I'm always filming at school. But God forbid you look tired or you have a pimple, because then everyone's like, oh, she's looking sloppy, what's going on?"

"Ah," Jasper said. "People think what they see is the only thing to see."

Izzy nodded. "Right, and I post stuff about school and beauty products and going out and stuff because people like it. Those are the kind of videos that get the most clicks. But there are other things I do that are cool too."

Izzy and Jasper walked downstairs back toward the kitchen. "Sometimes I think about shutting the whole channel down," Izzy said. "But it's so big now, I don't just want to quit."

Jasper looked at the photos on the walls, turning his head in thought. "You don't only have to post about school stuff just because your followers like it. Maybe you could change up the format, add more of what you like on the channel. Like your photography work. Poppy told you these photo shoots would create tons of footage for your blog. Try using some of it to see if your followers like it. Even if your current followers don't, maybe new followers will come on who do."

"You're right," Izzy said.

"Break your own rules, so to speak," Jasper said.

"A lot of my followers like when you're on my vlog," Izzy said.

"I didn't mean including me," Jasper said. "I meant your photography."

"Right, yes," Izzy said. "My photography work, yes. That's cool. But people still like you too."

Jasper rolled his eyes. "How do you know?"

"The comments are on fire. You should read them. Tons of girls always comment about how hot you are."

Jasper started to blush. "I thought that the first rule of being an Internet star was to never read the comments."

"True," she said. "But like you said, rules have to be broken once in a while."

· · ·

Zee sat in her usual chair during music theory class, attentively taking notes. Of all her classes, music theory was Zee's happy place. She even smiled during lecture, and not just because Archie sat right behind her. Though his presence did make her stomach flutter, at least a little.

Archie leaned forward in his chair during music theory, his face close to Zee's back. His mere presence challenged Zee's concentration, so when he whispered her name her focus was completely gone.

"Cali," he whispered. "You digging this lecture?"

"Yep," Zee said. "Are you paying attention?"

"Hard to pay attention when you're near, my dear," Archie smiled. Zee blushed. "Jam session today?"

Zee turned around. "I'm still not finished with my song."

"S'all right. Doesn't need to be perfect. Let's hear it. After class?"

Zee clenched her teeth. She had an appointment with her therapist this afternoon. "I can't. I have a meeting."

"Then text me a version of it. I want to hear it."

Zee agreed just so she could distract him from pursuing a meetup any further. " 'Kay."

Archie leaned back in his chair once again. Zee looked down and scribbled notes furiously to keep herself from being distracted again. Once the school bell rang, Archie dashed out the door without a word. Zee exhaled deeply, the flutters in her stomach settling still, and hoped that she was off the hook for having to send her unfinished lyrics to him.

• • •

Dr. Banks's office was starting to feel as familiar to Zee to as her own dorm room. The conversations between the therapist and the student had become more easygoing and natural. Zee almost looked forward to their meetings.

"The journaling has helped," Zee told Dr. Banks.

"Great," Dr. Banks said. "How so? Any new things you've noticed?"

Zee took a breath. "Well, writing every day has helped me brainstorm song lyrics."

"That's good," Dr. Banks said. "I'm excited to see you perform."

"You'll be there?" Zee asked.

"Of course. My husband and I go every year."

Zee nodded. *Great. Now I have to impress my therapist too.*

"Let's talk about your classes. How are those going?" Dr. Banks asked.

Zee shifted in her seat. "Depends on the class."

"Okay, let's go down your schedule. Algebra, how is that going?"

"Meh. I'm not rocking it, but not failing it right now."

"Do you think the work is too hard for you?"

"I think it's just not my favorite subject. It's pretty dry."

"I understand," Dr. Banks said. "What about science?"

"At least we're studying the oceans now, so I'm more interested. But when we did the circuitry study, I struggled."

"I see. English lit?"

"Mrs. Pender isn't the most exciting teacher," Zee said.

"How so?"

"Well, her voice just—I dunno, half the time I end up falling asleep in her class."

Dr. Banks took copious notes and nodded while Zee talked. "Do you find yourself daydreaming or looking off into space during class?"

"Yeah, my mind wanders when I'm bored," Zee said.

Dr. Banks smiled. "What classes are you not bored in?"

"The ones involving music and food."

Dr. Banks let out a small laugh. "That makes sense, Zee. Makes total sense."

At the end of their time, Zee and Dr. Banks confirmed their next session. Zee walked down the hallway past the offices toward the exit, feeling more relaxed than when she had arrived. Then a familiar voice called from behind. "Cali."

Zee froze as if she'd been caught eating ice cream straight out of the carton before turning around. "Um, Archie."

"Were you in with Dr. Banks?"

Zee fumbled for an explanation. "I, um, she asked me to see her."

"Right," Archie said, walking toward her. "You know, only the cool kids go to therapy. I've been going since I was seven."

Zee's eyes widened. "You have?"

Archie's face softened. "Heading home? I'm going that way."

The two walked toward the main exit leading out to the quad. Archie held the door open for Zee. She grabbed her bag tighter.

"So you go to a therapist here at school?" Zee asked.

"Me? No. I've been seeing the same one back at home since I was seven. Sometimes she travels with us on vacation. But yeah, she knows all about me. She's probably the reason why I still go to school."

"Really?"

"Well, she helped me realize that I had no choice but to go to school. I used to cut class all day. I was angry at my mum and dad, resented them for always being gone. Tried to become a human volcano with Alka-Seltzer."

"What?!" Zee responded.

"Yeah, it was dumb. I was eleven and took a bunch of antacids because I thought my stomach would explode. It didn't," Archie explained. "Banks is cool though. Not your typical stodgy therapist. You like her?"

"Yeah, she's really nice."

"So something is troubling you," Archie said, placing a hand on Zee's shoulder. "That sad song is about something in your life."

Zee looked down again. What went on in Dr. Banks's office was not something she wanted to share. "I'm fine now. She's just giving me some pointers on how to handle some stress."

"Ah," Archie said. "So, you going to perform that song you played for me?"

Zee looked at him, reluctant to sing her incomplete song for him. She saw a bench nearby and nodded toward it. "Let me just sing the rest for you here. I don't have that much more."

"I don't have my guitar on me."

"Hum the melody. You just wanted lyrics anyway."

The two walked over to the bench near the end of the

quad. It was across from a group of students playing soccer and another group gossiping about classes. Zee took out her journal and opened it to the page with her lyrics. She cleared her throat, took a breath, and started singing:

> "Waiting, wondering, fading from your eye
> Hard to catch you, no matter how hard I try
> Never meant to hurt you..."

Archie stared firmly at her until she finished. "I have to say, Cali, I haven't known you that long and all, but this just... doesn't sound like you."

"What?" Zee said. "But you put the perfect guitar riff to it earlier."

"I know, I know," Archie said. "But looking at you, looking at you out here on the school grounds with this overcast sky. You're the sunshine in these gray clouds. Do you know why I call you Cali? Because you're fresh. You're bright. You sparkle. And like, I think you should inject a bit of that into what you're singing about."

Zee looked down, confused. *He didn't like the song,* she thought, *but he has all of these nice things to say about me. Fresh? Sparkling?*

"Look, I'm not saying the song isn't good," Archie said. "I'm saying the song's not you. Not right now." He put his hand on her shoulder, then whispered in her ear. "Write from your heart, Cali."

Archie planted a kiss on her cheek, and got up from the bench and walked away.

Zee sat on the bench alone, her pensive face staring after

Archie. She was heartbroken about her song being rejected. But the hard blow of rejection was cushioned by a kiss on the cheek and being called sunny and sparkling by the pensive and rebellious Archie Saint John.

11

HARSH CRITIC

There were just a few weeks left before the Festival, and every day Jameela had been putting in long hours to improve her ballet. Her instructor, Ms. Duckett, had been critical of her body and her form, but between eating only salads and training harder than ever, Jameela unintentionally lost a few pounds and gained more flexibility in her limbs. She choreographed a classical piece from *Swan Lake* with a slightly modern interpretation. After weeks of practice, Ms. Duckett gave her a weak compliment: "Your toes look better. Pointier. Keep it up." Jameela used the halfhearted remarks to fuel her drive for perfection even more.

As Jameela walked into her dorm room after a long day of classes and dance, she overheard Zee singing at her desk. "What is that droll-sounding tune?" Jameela said.

Zee looked startled as Jameela watched her, waiting for the answer. "It's my song for the Festival," Zee said.

"It sounds dreadful," Jameela scoffed. "Did I hear something about running down a path to destruction?"

"No, that's not what I said," Zee replied. "The song is about missed connections. It's an acoustic number. Since I'm doing a solo performance, I don't need a big band."

"Well, you're going to put the crowd to sleep. You might want to reconsider."

Zee felt a fire in her belly growing hotter as she stood there. The fire spread to her arms and legs, and then her throat. She couldn't fight it back anymore.

"Listen, Jameela, I don't make fun of you dancing on your toes to some corny flutes and whistles in a frilly skirt, so why are you poking fun at my music? If it's not your type of vibe, fine! But respect my vibe. I respect yours."

Zee stormed out of the room before Jameela could say anything more.

Jameela stood motionless in front of her mirror. She had never heard Zee be so stern with her, even when Jameela kept missing curfew to do ballet. She blinked a few times, standing in front of her dresser, breathless. Then she smiled. Maybe Zee wasn't this clueless, soft little girl that Jameela had assumed she was. Maybe she had a stronger backbone than she thought. *Wow, she stood up for herself,* Jameela thought. *Much respect to that, if not to that awful song.*

But, Jameela wondered, *where all of a sudden was this confidence coming from?*

• • •

In the bathroom, Zee bent over the sink and splashed water against her cheeks repeatedly, letting the cool water calm her down. She stared at the mirror, feeling the pressure behind her temples release as the water dripped down her face.

Taking a few deep belly breaths, Zee walked back to her room slightly calmer, but not in the mood to be near Jameela. When she opened the door, she saw Jameela standing in between their beds. "I was just about to change my clothes," Jameela said nervously.

Zee's computer was still open on her desk. Her desktop had a scene of a sunset in what looked like the California coast, with folders all around the perimeter, somewhat organized to at least keep the sun and most of the bay in view. Zee snapped it shut, then grabbed her journal and walked out of the room to the lounge downstairs. *Maybe I could find more crowd-*

pleasing lyrics if I sat with other people, she thought.

• • •

Settling into a corner chair in the common lounge of the dorm, Zee flipped open her laptop again. The hum of other kids chatting, watching television, playing ping-pong, and studying was a welcome background noise—it drowned out the noise of Zee's racing thoughts.

A message notification from the Zee Files popped up on her laptop from Chloe: *How was therapy?*

Zee opened the message and a photo of Chloe in two Dutch braids popped up with the caption: *How was therapy? Decided to go with this for soccer sectionals. Should last a week rain or shine, win or lose. Very Instagram fitness influencer, riiiiight?*

Zee responded with two thumbs-up emojis, then wrote back: *It was interesting. The session itself was fine, but Archie saw me after when I was leaving. Now he knows I go to therapy. But he told me he goes to therapy too! Maybe I should rock those braids for my Festival performance. Conference call soon?*

Chloe wrote back: *See? Therapy is for the cool kids. Let's try this weekend for a call. Love you.*

Zee leaned back from her computer. *Thank goodness for Chloe,* Zee thought. *My own sunshine on an otherwise gray day.*

12

NOT PICTURED

Moe's Coffee Shop was already abuzz when Izzy and Poppy set up at their favorite table, pulling out books and notes from class. It wasn't one of their scheduled study dates with the gang, but they both were craving Moe's famous golden turmeric chai lattes, so they went. "We only have an hour because I've got to meet Mr. Hysworth about my exhibition," Izzy said.

They sipped their frothy lattes and started going through their notes. A few minutes later, Poppy's phone rang. She looked down at the screen. "Ah, my sister's calling from New York. I better take this. Sorry, I'll be back."

Poppy headed toward the exit, reaching for the door just as Jasper was walking in. They exchanged nods, and Jasper made his way toward the register to order.

"Jasper! Hey!" Izzy called out to him.

"Hey!" Jasper had planned to get a quick cup of tea on his way to pick up some sound equipment, but Izzy's presence was a pleasant detour.

"I have a surprise for you," Izzy teased as he came over.

"A surprise?" Jasper asked.

Izzy turned around to her bag and reached for a folder. She handed it to Jasper. Inside were a handful of selected photos from the photo shoot last week—close-up portraits, action shots of Jasper running or jumping, laughing photos showing Jasper's lovely smile. Jasper had never seen himself look so good on film. "Wow, Izzy, this... it's me?"

"Of course! You look great! I'm so excited to frame the finals," Izzy said, taking the photos back and slowly flipping through the images. "Ooh, look at that one."

"What? Where I'm jumping? I look like a madman there."

"No, there's so much life in that one. I'm going to show them to Mr. Hysworth in a bit and we'll pick the ones we'll display for the exhibit."

The two pointed at the photos, critiquing and laughing as they went through them. Izzy seemed proud of her photographs of Jasper. And Jasper, stepping out of the shadows for a rare moment in the spotlight, felt honored to have been one of Izzy's models.

· · ·

Zee was heading to pick up a few things from the stationers, but when she walked past Moe's along the way, a craving for a turmeric latte bubbled in her belly. She entered the coffee shop as Poppy stood near the front window on the phone and Zee immediately heard Jasper's laughter from the left side. She looked over and saw Jasper and Izzy talking closely at a corner table. Zee hadn't expected them to be meeting alone.

Zee walked over to their table. "Hi," Zee said. Izzy and Jasper stopped laughing to look up at her. "Am I interrupting something?"

"Zee, wow, what a coincidence," Izzy said. "The gang's all here. Come sit, we're just going over something."

Zee froze. Jasper's face went from happy to surprised, but then he quickly went back to looking at the photos he was holding.

"This looks like a private study season," Zee said. "I didn't know you guys met without me."

"We don't. Poppy's out front taking a phone call. And I happened to run into Jasper," Izzy said. "I was showing Jasper my Festival project."

Jasper was so enthralled by the photos he barely looked up at Zee. "Yeah, I just wanted tea. Izzy, these are just so spectacular," he said.

Zee's chest felt hollow. Suddenly, that familiar throbbing at the temples returned. She knew that Izzy was into him. She could tell by the way Izzy leaned into him and how she looked at his mouth when she spoke. And now, these two sitting here, fawning over Izzy's work, confirmed how close the bond between Izzy and Jasper had grown. The type of bond that Zee had with Jasper at one point, but now it felt like that bond was slipping away.

"You know, I'm going to head back," Zee heard herself say, though she didn't really want to bolt so quickly. "I've got an appointment and need to study. I'll see you guys later."

Jasper looked up. "You don't want to stay and study a bit? Since we're all here?"

"I should head back. I've got dinner plans," Zee lied, wanting to escape as quickly as possible.

Zee walked quickly toward the exit and pushed herself through the door, blinking hard as the autumn air blew back in her face. She was ready to run all the way home, but only made it a few paces toward the street corner when a red light forced her to wait at the stoplight. Jasper was a few paces behind her.

"Zee, wait up," he called. "I can walk you back to the dorm."

Zee stopped and turned toward Jasper. "So like, what, you two are best friends now?"

"We're *all* friends. She was just showing me her Festival portraits. She took my photos last week."

"Wait," Zee said. "She took your photos?"

"Yeah, she took my photos for her Festival project. She's doing up close and personal portraits of our classmates."

"She didn't ask for my portrait," Zee said.

"Maybe she's going to ask you soon," Jasper replied.

"The Festival is in a few weeks now. She must be almost done with her presentation."

"She just photographed me last week at her house, so there's still time."

"Wait." Zee stepped away from Jasper. "You've been to her *house* now?"

"Yeah," Jasper replied. "I mean, it's only a half hour away. What's the big deal?"

Zee didn't know how to digest all this information. She had assumed she and Jasper would have spent much more time together by now, but outside of studying and class time they hadn't done anything else. Now it seemed he was spending more time with Izzy than with her. Zee felt like she was losing her only good friend on campus. And it made her feel even more disconnected to her new surroundings.

"Nothing, Jasper. That's cool that she included you. I'm sure the photos look awesome," Zee said.

Jasper shrugged. "Well, beauty is in the eye of the beholder, so we'll see. How's your song coming along? I have some ideas for it if you want to get together to work on it. Tomorrow?"

Zee had therapy tomorrow. "Um, we'll see. My schedule's packed. Check in tomorrow?"

"Now you're blowing me off?"

The red light turned green, and Zee started walking away from him to cross the street. "Sorry. Let's do one day this week for sure. I'll text you later," she called.

Zee shuffled off toward the stationers, regretting her detour into Moe's for that tasty but unnecessary turmeric latte. Today that frothy beverage just proved to be more trouble than it was worth.

• • •

The Jasper and Izzy spotting at Moe's left Zee unsettled. She left a message for Chloe and Ally in the Zee Files: *Ladies. Urgent call needed. Can we plan a conference call soon?*

By the next afternoon, the three arranged a time to chat while Chloe got ready for school and Zee and Ally were already home from class.

"But they were, like, *together* at the table," Zee wailed to the girls. "Looking at photos! Being, like, cute and stuff!"

"But he said there was nothing going on," Ally said.

"Yeah."

" 'Kay, so..."

"Sounds like they just happened to be getting lattes at the same time. Those turmeric lattes are that good, huh?" Chloe said.

"They are pretty great," Zee said. "But here's the deal. Jasper gave me all this grief about hanging out with Archie, and now he's hanging out with Izzy Matthews, YouTube star. Did he forget *we* were friends?"

"Maybe he's only hanging out with her because you're spending so much time with Archie," Ally said.

"I'm not spending *that* much time. I haven't even seen him in a week or so. Anyway." Zee took a breath. "Am I'm overreacting?"

"Yes," Ally and Chloe said simultaneously.

"I just thought we'd end up spending more time together and he'd really help show me around school and London. But that's not happening."

"Well, you did run out on him at the coffee shop," Ally said. "Maybe you should tell him how you're feeling."

"So what, say, 'I'm jealous you're hanging out with the school celebrity and I want you to hang out with me instead'?"

"If that's how you feel, it's a start," Ally said.

"All right, ladies, I gotta jump. School calls," Chloe said. "Message me later and let me know the latest." Chloe dropped off, leaving Ally and Zee to chat alone.

"How's everything with you?" Zee asked Ally.

"It's going. My dad is not here, naturally."

"Is he at the office?"

"Or out on assignment, who knows? He usually makes it in time for dinner and brings back takeout or something for us to eat."

"Are you home alone after school every day?"

Ally shook her head. "No, most days I'm at school until about 4:30 or 5 p.m. and we meet at home. But today we have a free day from the journal, so I'm here. Alone."

"Ah, gotcha. So how are things at home?" Zee asked.

"Things are okay. My mom called the other day upset about something again, so they had an argument. I heard screaming and something about spending too much money. But whatever, I put my headphones on and try to block out that yelling when I need to."

"Whoa. I'm sorry, Ally."

"Yeah, it's okay. More fun to hear about your adventures. I

have to get some homework in though. Keep us posted on this love triangle you've found yourself in."

"Ha, very funny," Zee said. "Miss you." Then they left the conference call.

Zee tapped her finger on the desk next to the keyboard, mimicking the beat of Archie's guitar riff and humming to herself as she stared out of the window. She thought about Jasper again. *Should I tell him how I feel?* she wondered.

13

AN OPEN BOOK

Zee was feeling nostalgic. Since her computer was open, she went online to see what the weather was like back at Brookdale. Then she went to Brookdale Academy's website and checked out their news releases, updated gallery photos ("Ooh there's Chloe in the news lab," Zee said), and sports results from recent games. She spotted her old music teacher Mr. P in a photo of the band practicing on campus. Then her mind was jostled by a photo of one of the drummers carrying an old book.

Book, Zee thought. She closed her computer and looked around her room for her old journal, the one with the tie-dye cover. It was her songwriting notebook from Brookdale, packed with one-liners, choruses, and verses she often jotted down in messy handwriting as fast as they popped into her mind. She had tossed the old journal in her bag at the last minute when she was packing up to come back to campus from her London home.

Zee found the notebook in one of her suitcases and flipped

through the tattered pages, glancing at the lyrics she'd written down during happier times at Brookdale. *Everybody gets a party and my party gets cupcakes and you,* said one.

That's almost too sweet for even me, Zee thought.

Twenty pages into the journal, she flipped to a page with the title "Open Book." Zee had written a near-complete song that she had played back at Brookdale. She read through the lyrics.

> *What do you see? It matters how you look.*
> *It's just me. I'm an open book.*
> *We're all scared, trying to hide,*
> *Keeping secrets inside...*

It's just me, Zee thought. She felt a fluttering in her chest.

> *Read me. Read me.*
> *I'm an open book.*
> *Take more than just one look.*

Zee sang the lyrics to the melody Archie came up with on his guitar. *This could work. This would work much better than what I had before,* she thought.

She reached for her cell phone and texted Jasper.

Zee

> Can you meet today? I just got a genius idea for my song! Same melody, better song.

This afternoon. Music hall?
Recording studio?

Recording studio. See you then!

• • •

"Wow, Zee, this is more... you," Jasper said after he heard Zee's new song in the recording studio.

"Right? Not as heavy as before," Zee said.

"What sparked the change?"

"I found this in my old notebook from Brookdale," she said. "Once I sang the hook, something inside me just felt right. Like this was the right song to sing, right now."

"I think the hook will work great. We can add a little piano in here, and it'll sound great," Jasper said. He played a short piano riff from a clip on his computer.

"OH-my-*lanta*!" Zee squealed. "This is it!" *It's just me... I'm an open book. Read me. Read me.* The word "me" ended the song on an uplifting note.

"Perfect!" Zee squealed "I love it!"

"Yep," Jasper said. He turned to Zee, smiling. "Nice working with you again."

Zee turned back toward him. She felt a lightness in her body she hadn't felt since rehearsals with The Beans. "This is great, Jas," Zee said, excited. "I missed this. It feels like old times in Brookdale."

"It does, doesn't it?" Jasper said. "You can always ask me

for help any time."

"I know... I just..." Zee struggled to find the right words to explain that she felt he had pulled away from her in favor of more time with Izzy.

"It's okay," Jasper said, clicking his mousepad on his laptop. "Shall we play it back to hear how it all sounds?"

"Yes!"

Jasper cued up the song from the beginning and let it play from the loudspeakers. Zee smiled as she bopped her head, envisioning herself singing the song on the stage, working the crowd from left to right. It was an uplifting poppy tune, something that would make even Jameela's tightly wound shoulders bob up and down.

"It's great, Zee," Jasper said. "You'll make a strong debut at the Festival."

"I'm nervous," Zee said, eyes wide.

"Ah, don't be. I'll be in the sound booth, so I'll make sure everything sounds on point."

Zee swayed side to side, mouthing the words to the beat, and for the first time in weeks, she actually felt excited to perform in front of her therapist, her teachers, and the very talented student body of The Hollows Creative Arts Academy.

14

SHOWTIME

Zee had not heard such a loud roar in the concert hall ever. At least, not in person. But on the night of the annual Creative Arts Festival, hundreds of parents, teachers, students, and friends gathered in the concert hall, eager to watch and hear the artistic talents of The Hollows student body.

The special event was scheduled late Friday afternoon to allow parents an opportunity to come check out their kids' performances. It also allowed students to have the choice to head back home with their parents for the weekend after a long week of practice and rehearsals.

Mr. and Mrs. Carmichael drove together to campus to see their daughter's first major performance since moving to London. Mr. Carmichael picked up his wife from home, leaving the twins behind with Camilla. Mrs. Carmichael posted live updates for her social media feed as they rode to The Hollows. She used #stagemom as a caption to a photo of herself and Mr. Carmichael walking into the concert hall.

When they arrived, the Carmichaels walked through a long hallway full of portraits by Izzy Matthews as they meandered to the auditorium. They chose seats in the middle of the theater so they could have a full view of the stage. As they sat down, the Chapmans, Jasper's parents, who sat a few rows over toward the left side of the stage, saw them and waved hello to the Carmichaels.

Near the front of the stage were Mr. and Mrs. Chopra, Jameela's parents. Every year that Jameela has performed at the Festival, they have sat in the third row on the left side of the stage to cheer their daughter on. On the other side of the auditorium, the Anands, Tom's parents, sat in the front row near the aisle.

Zee paced backstage between other performers, trying to claim a small space to be with her thoughts. Nervous excitement pounded against the walls of her chest. She sang the words to the song to herself. *"It's just me..."*

"Hey," a familiar voice interrupted her thoughts. It was Jasper, with a clipboard in hand. He spoke fast as if he were in a hurry. "Break a leg out there. I'll be watching from the booth. You can look at me in between the two floors of the auditorium if you want to picture a familiar face smiling back at you. But I'm sure your parents are out there somewhere, so maybe you don't need me."

"Jas," Zee said. "I'll always welcome your friendly face. And thank you."

Jasper smiled and nodded. "I'll see you after the show," he said, and hurried off to the sound booth.

As the auditorium lights went down, the school band played a short piece to begin the big event. The crowd gave a hearty welcome, whooping and clapping as the band finished.

"Good afternoon, everyone. Welcome to the fifty-third annual Creative Arts Festival. We are so excited to have you all here," Mr. Hysworth said to the crowd in his booming intro. "Tonight, we have a stellar lineup for you all. From song to dance to theatrical one-person performances, we've got something for everyone. Let's start the show!"

• • •

Tom took the stage wearing a white T-shirt and white linen pants, and sat cross-legged on the floor. He placed a small set of bongos in between his legs. "Greetings, everyone!" he said. "I wanted to give you all something to put some good vibes out in the world."

He sang words that didn't sound quite like any language Zee recognized. He hit the bongo drum gently to enhance every other word or so, then ended the song with the longest "ohm" she ever heard before.

Tom then went into an original poem about the union of mankind and taking care of our planet. "Loving the earth—our home—number one—every being—every creature—every mother—every son." He drummed fast on the bongo, then finally he brought the palms of his hands together in front of his chest. The crowd quietly clapped, some confused about what they just saw, others inspired by the unique performance. The applause built as Tom gathered his bongos, stood up, and walked carefully off the stage.

Jameela's performance came after Tom's. As Tom walked backstage, he saw Jameela standing in her pink leotard and pointe shoes. Her lips were pursed together and she looked straight ahead, concentrating on her upcoming dance. But her skin glowed and her limbs moved gracefully as she quickly went through her routine. Tom stopped in front of her. An involuntary smile grew across his face. "You'll do great," he said.

Startled out of her thoughts, Jameela turned to Tom. She relaxed her body and smiled back. "Thank you," she said. A small pause grew between them. "I watched you from backstage. I really liked your performance."

"Yeah?" Tom said, raising an eyebrow.

"Yeah," Jameela said. "The bongos brought it all to another level. Really great."

"Thank you," Tom said. "You'll kill it out there."

"If I can just keep my balance on these shoes," she joked.

The two grinned at each other, then bashfully looked away. Tom turned back to her. "I'm going to go out there so I can see you better. Balance is easy to find if you just breathe." He turned and walked away, leaving Jameela smiling behind him.

Mr. Hysworth took the stage once again. "Our next performer is one of The Hollows's best ballet dancers and has been a star student of Ms. Duckett. Please welcome Jameela Chopra!"

Jameela floated across the stage as classical music played behind her. She glided from pliés to jumps and turns, her limbs moving like light sheaths of ribbon. Tom stood near the front of the stage, mesmerized by her movements. Zee was backstage, prepping to perform after her, but was also stunned by her roommate's grace. Jameela's face changed to match the mood of the piece, somber at times, then strong and determined. She ended with what seemed like endless turns on her left toes, her body rotating around like a top, until she gracefully landed her right foot back behind her. Then as the music came to an end, she moved forward and bowed to the audience.

The applause roared through the auditorium, her classmates rising to their feet to cheer for Jameela's performance. Jameela's parents stayed seated in the third row, her stoic father applauding politely, her mother jumping to her feet at the end of the last note, clapping her hands feverishly and whistling.

Jameela walked off the stage. Tom was the first person she saw. He stood there applauding, then bowed. "That. Was. Beautiful."

For the first time in a long time, Jameela felt happy after a performance, the kind of joy she used to feel when she was younger, before medals and competitions, before "the change." It was nice to see a friendly face like Tom's when she came off stage.

"I remembered to breathe," she replied, smiling.

• • •

Zee rocked back and forth on her feet, working out the nervous energy built up in her body. She knew following Jameela would be tough, but she wondered if the crowd would think she was as engaging as her roommate. *And is Archie out there?* Zee wondered. She hadn't seen him before the show, and she also hadn't seen his name on the show program.

Zee started to repeat some affirmations like Tom

suggested during their cooking class. "I am talented. I am creative. I have something to say and share." She closed her eyes and repeated each of them a few times.

"Zee!" Jameela's voice broke her concentration. "You ready for your first Festival performance?"

"Yes. I guess," Zee said.

Jameela smiled at Zee. "You'll do great. I'm super proud of you. Takes a lot of courage to get up in front of a stage at a new school in front of new people and sing by yourself. But you've done it before, so I know you'll be fine."

Zee was surprised at the pep talk from her roommate who had been so critical in the weeks leading up to the Festival. "Thanks. Whew. There's a big crowd out there, right?"

Jameela nodded. "Yeah, but don't think about them. Think about me and Tom and Jasper and Archie smiling backstage for you. Right?"

Zee nodded. *Archie. I wonder where he is?* She smiled back at Jameela. "Thank you."

Jameela brought both of her hands to Zee's shoulders and gave them a squeeze. "You've got this."

Mr. Hysworth returned to the stage, taking the mic as the crowd settled back into their seats. "All right, everyone, our next performer is one of our newest students here at The Hollows, and one of our international students. She is a year nine student from California and is a wonderful singer and songwriter. Today she's singing an original song she's written. Please welcome Mackenzie Carmichael!"

Zee walked onto the stage and took the mic from Mr. Hysworth. When she had walked onto the stage before the Festival, it felt big and cavernous. Now, with Tom and Jameela backstage, Jasper sitting in the control room queuing up a track he arranged for her, and her parents in the crowd, she didn't feel so alone. She stood still in the middle of the stage, took a breath, closed her eyes, and waited for the music to start.

The words flowed out of her body like a rainbow, colorful and light. She looked directly at the crowd, finding a friendly face to sing the first line, then finding another face for the second. She moved across the stage, her right hand on her heart, smiling to the audience, singing each line of the song to one person as she went, locking in a personal connection to her audience.

> *"What do you see? It matters how you look.*
> *It's just me. I'm an open book.*
> *We're all scared, trying to hide,*
> *Keeping secrets inside...*
> *Not me! I've tried, but I'm an open book.*
> *Read me. Read me.*
> *I'm an open book."*

Jameela stood on the side of the stage, not blinking once since Zee took the stage. Tom smiled and nodded his head with the music. Zee's friends looked at each other and gave an approving nod to one another. "Yup, that's our girl," Tom said.

Zee came back to the center of the stage and hit the last notes of the song, staring deeply into the audience, finding a person in the middle of the crowd to connect with. Then the lights went down and thunderous applause grew across the crowd. "Whoooo!"

The lights came back up. Zee smiled and waved to the

audience, skipping over to the side of the stage. Tom and Jameela were there waiting for her. "Great job, mate," Tom said, sticking his fist out toward her for a fist bump. "Truly great."

Zee tapped his fist. "Thank you. The affirmations helped!"

"I can tell."

Jameela put her arms around Zee, hugging her. "That was amazing, Zee. Really, really amazing!"

Zee had never seen Jameela be so excited about anything. She hugged her back, grateful for the tender display of support.

"Wow, thank you, Jameela. That means a lot coming from you."

Zee felt happy, like she used to feel after performances with The Beans back in California. As she walked backstage to gather her things, students from other years called out to her. "That was great!" "Wow! Do you have a YouTube channel?" "You should release a record!" "Hey, can you sing at my birthday party?" Zee felt like she was finally an insider in the new world she'd arrived in a few months prior.

No matter what happened from here, whether she did perform at that kid's birthday party (*What was his name again?* Zee wondered) or a talent scout recruited her for West End theater productions, the joy of seeing her peers connect to a song she wrote from the heart was the only validation she needed to feel good about her talent and her place within The Hollows.

15

THE CROWD GOES WILD

here you are!" Zee heard a voice behind her. It was deeper than a woman's, but it wasn't Archie. Zee's head whipped around and saw her parents behind her. Her father stretched his arms out toward her, then pulled her in close. "So proud of you, honey!"

"Aww, thanks, Dad!" Zee hugged him back.

Mrs. Carmichael beamed. "That was great! I took video of it for my IG stories. I tagged you in them. Did you get the notifications?"

"I haven't looked at my phone in a while," Zee admitted.

"Ah, right. You were kind of busy. You looked amazing on stage! Was that song about yourself?" her mother asked. Zee shrugged her shoulders coyly.

Mrs. Carmichael's head turned around quickly as if she were trying to take everything in at once, but her eyes weren't moving fast enough. "Look at these talented kids! Did you see that one guy's theater piece? Really moving. Oh! Is that Izzy Matthews over there talking to Jasper?"

Zee's head turned. There they were again. Together. It was an event, but they were talking as if no one else were in the room. "I'm going to go ask her if I can get a photo with her for my IG feed," Mrs. Carmichael said. "Hold on."

Zee watched her mother flit away. "So everyone is more interested in Izzy Matthews than me?" Zee asked no one in particular.

"What's that?" Mr. Carmichael said.

"Nothing," Zee said.

"How are you feeling?" her father asked.

"I feel great, now that the Festival show is done."

"Great," Mr. Carmichael said, putting his hand on her shoulder. "Shall we look around? These pictures of the students here are really good."

As Zee and her father took in Izzy's photo exhibit, Zee felt a pang of jealousy at not being included in Izzy's collection. Then, Dr. Banks, wearing a leather jacket, a white blouse, and wide-legged black trousers, walked toward her. "Zee!" she called out, holding her husband's hand. "Hi, I've been looking for you! Congratulations!"

"Thanks," Zee said.

"This is my husband, Tyler Banks," Dr. Banks introduced. Mr. Banks's white teeth were perfectly straight and a dimple in his left cheek appeared when he smiled. He reached out his hand to introduce himself.

"Nice to meet you," Mr. Banks said to Zee. "Yes, your song was lovely. Really touching."

"Thanks so much," Zee said, looking at Mr. Banks. He wore a well-tailored navy suit, but kept his jacket unbuttoned. He was not wearing a tie. *Is this what they mean by business casual in London?* Zee wondered.

Dr. Banks turned to Mr. Carmichael. "Mr. Carmichael, nice to see you."

Mr. Carmichael shook her hand. "Yes, indeed, how are you? How's my Zee been doing?"

"She's great. I think she's really going to enjoy herself here the more time she spends at The Hollows."

"Well, I think she just needs to remember why she was chosen to be a part of this very selective school, right?" Mr. Carmichael said, looking at Zee.

"Indeed," Dr. Banks replied.

As Dr. Banks and Mr. Carmichael talked, Zee caught her mother's eye from across the foyer. Zee quickly interrupted her dad's conversation with Dr. Banks. "Dad, can we get some water?"

"Sure, honey," Mr. Carmichael said. He turned to Dr. Banks. "Nice to see you. I'll email you next week." Zee grabbed her father's hand and they scooted away from Dr. Banks.

Mrs. Carmichael met up with her family at the refreshments table. "Who was that you were talking with, honey?"

"Thanks for my water," Zee said, trying to distract her mom.

"I'll introduce you later, darling. Let's go take a look at these student portraits," Mr. Carmichael said.

• • •

Izzy's photo exhibit was a beautiful focal point for the grand entrance of the concert hall. Students flocked around to check out their framed portraits, and those who were not photographed enjoyed looking for their friends and reading the short bio that hung with each image. Parents gazed at the artful portraits of their children, and Izzy walked around the room taking video of the scene for her YouTube channel.

Jasper's photograph hung prominently at the end of the main entrance to the room. His classic features looked even more handsome blown up to poster size, and his smile was as bright as one of the overhead lights. Jasper, who had spent the entire Festival show in the sound booth, met his parents in front of his photo.

"It's silly, right?" Jasper said.

"Not anything of the sort!" Mrs. Chapman said. "You look dashing here! I want a copy for myself. Where's the photographer?"

Izzy, with camera in hand, approached the family from behind. "Hello!" she said. "Jasper, it looks better in person, right?"

"It looks bigger, that's for sure," Jasper said.

Izzy introduced herself to the Chapmans. "Can I film you all for my YouTube channel?" she asked.

"Absolutely!" Mrs. Chapman beamed. "This is simply fantastic." They hammed it up the camera. "Wait, get my good side," Mr. Chapman joked.

"All right," Izzy said. "Tell me what you really think about your son's photo."

"I think he looks amazing, and I think you're an amazing photographer," Mrs. Chapman said directly to the camera. Jasper's cheeks became pink and rosy as his mother gushed on.

"Ah, great, thank you!" Izzy said, nudging Jasper with her

elbow. "This is good content here!"

"My parents on YouTube? Great. More embarrassing than seeing myself on camera," Jasper said.

Izzy placed her hand on Jasper's forearm. "Jasper, you look fantastic. See what happens when you step out from behind the scenes?"

Jasper looked at the photo. He looked happy, but distinguished. Mature, but with a boyish charm. Izzy was good at bringing out the best spirit of each of the students on film.

"I still like my place out of the spotlight," Jasper said.

"Well," Izzy said, and planted a kiss on his cheek. "Sometimes it's good to break your own rules."

16

PICTURE PERFECT

*Z*ee looked around the walls of the concert hall at the beautiful portraits shot by Izzy. Izzy had taken more than a hundred portraits of students from various levels and included short interviews with a few of them and memorable quotes from the others. Then Zee saw Jasper's portrait hanging on the wall. *Wow, he looks really handsome there. And look, there's Jameela looking poised and beautiful,* Zee thought to herself as she walked down the corridor. She spotted Poppy's photograph just beyond the second entrance. *Everyone looks amazing.*

Then she rounded the corner. "Oh. My. Lanta!" Zee said.

There, near the entrance to the center section of the theater, hung a photo that left her speechless. It was a side profile shot of a girl with curly hair, freckles, and wide eyes looking off into the distance. Zee stood in front of her. The caption card read: *Mackenzie Blue Carmichael. Year Nine. Originally from California. A breath of fresh air at The Hollows.*

"Surprise!" Izzy said from the side of the wall. She had her camera around her neck and held it up to Zee's face to record her reaction. "Did you really think I wasn't going to include you?"

"But..." Zee said, eyes still fixed on the photo. "When did you take this?"

"A few weeks back," Izzy said. "You were sitting on that bench by yourself, and as soon as I saw your profile I just knew I had to snap the shot. I was going to show you when I took the photo, but you got up and trotted away too fast for me to

catch up. Then I had Mr. Hysworth reach out to your parents to grant permission to use the photo. And they agreed."

The Carmichaels came up behind them. "There it is! Oh my, it's beautiful, Zee," Mrs. Carmichael said, filming the scene with her cell phone to post to her feed.

Zee was stunned. Everything about the photo was brilliant. Her hair was shiny and full, her skin was glowing, and her eyes looked like hopeful, excited for whatever the future held. *I look like a model*, Zee thought. "I had no idea! I can't believe you did this."

"Do you like it?" Izzy asked. "It's my favorite one of all of the photos."

"Like it?" Zee said, hugging Izzy. "I love it!"

"Oh, good!" Izzy said, backing away to film Zee's overjoyed reaction. "I thought you might be annoyed I took it without telling you."

"No, but I did think I would be the only one of our year nine to be excluded from the exhibit."

"Oh, no way," Izzy said. "The only person I'm missing is Archie."

Archie.

It's official. Zee thought. *Archie Saint John has disappeared.*

Disappeared from the performance lineup of the Festival show. Disappeared from the lineup for Izzy Mathew's photo exhibit. And now, by the looks of the crowd starting to thin out in the concert hall, Archie Saint John was missing from the entire Creative Arts Festival for The Hollows this year.

· · ·

After mingling, hugging, smiling, and posing for selfies and photos for social media, Zee crawled into the back of a black SUV and headed home with her parents. She was relieved to finally have that over and looked forward to crashing in her own bed back in Notting Hill. As her head started to drift over toward the backseat window, her phone buzzed. A text message notification blared across the screen in the dark.

Archie

> Congrats, Cali. You killed it.

17

NEW (GIRL)FRIENDS

Zee spent the weekend at home, snuggling her twin siblings and sleeping in late after working so hard for her Festival performance. Her mother kept reviewing her videos of Zee's performance, proud of her daughter. "I can't believe you ever doubted yourself after all that time with The Beans. You've always been a star performer."

"Thanks for the seventeenth time, Mom," Zee said, laughing. "But I like the compliments, so keep 'em coming."

Camilla made a batch of sticky toffee buns to celebrate, and on Saturday Zee walked around her Notting Hill neighborhood with her mom and the twins, taking the toddlers to a local park to enjoy the playground. While there, one of Mrs. Carmichael's Mummy Mum friends, Sophie Raymond, impeccably dressed in a leather jacket and maxi dress with embroidered detailing along the seams, walked across the park toward the playground.

"Hello, darling!" Mrs. Carmichael said, giving the woman a kiss on the cheek.

"Hello, darling," Sophie said. "I see you've brought the family."

"Yes, this is my daughter, Zee. She's home this weekend from school."

The woman looked Zee up and down. "Zee, lovely to meet you. Your mother talks about you all the time."

"Thanks, I hope good things. Nice to meet you."

"Where are the kids?" Mrs. Carmichael asked Sophie.

"At home. I had to do some shopping and I didn't want to be distracted."

Sophie switched her attention to Mrs. Carmichael, and the two became engrossed in conversation. Zee turned back to the twins, making sure they got up and down the small slides and wood playset safely.

"Are you coming to tea on Tuesday?" Sophia asked Mrs. Carmichael. "Caroline will be there. Did you know she works for Burberry? Maybe you can chat about your 'gram to her and you can do something together."

"Yes, of course!" Mrs. Carmichael said, her eyes widening. "Wouldn't miss it."

"Great, see you then." Sophie walked off, and Mrs. Carmichael finally rejoined Zee and the twins at the bottom of the slide.

"So she's your friend?" Zee asked her mom.

"Yes, we get together once a week."

"Do the kids play together?"

"Oh, the kids don't come with us when we meet, honey," Mrs. Carmichael said. "It's a time where we moms can catch up alone. Sometimes it's the only alone time we get all week."

Zee looked at her siblings. "So it's a time where you can

run away from the kids to hang out?"

"No, silly!" Mrs. Carmichael said. "It's more a time where we get together and swap notes on what's going on with our kids and give each other advice or just talk about stuff."

"I see," Zee said, raising an eyebrow. *Mom friends who never hang out with their kids?* Zee thought.

Mrs. Carmichael grabbed Phoebe and Connor as they both came down the slide together giggling, Connor sitting behind Phoebe and grabbing her waist. "Wheeee! That was fun, right?" Mrs. Carmichael said. Zee watched as her mom pulled out her phone, held it out in front of them, and snapped a selfie for her Instagram feed.

• • •

On Saturday afternoon, Zee, Chloe, and Ally hopped on a conference call to recap all that went down during the Festival. Zee talked excitedly, happy to connect with her old friends.

"OMG," Chloe started. "I saw your portrait in Izzy Matthew's photo exhibit on her YouTube channel! Hello, boarding school gorge! The side-profile action shot? It was very Ralph Lauren American girl chic."

Zee beamed. "Thanks, Chloe!"

"Wait, I haven't seen it," Ally said. "Can you send us a copy or something?"

"I don't have one," Zee said.

"See if Izzy can get you a high-res version of it. Otherwise I'll get a screen grab from the video," Chloe said. "So, how did the rest of the Festival go?"

"It was mega!" Zee said. "I found an old song from my

Beans notebook and adapted it for my performance."

"I saw some clips on your mother's Instagram," Chloe said.

"Yeah, she was sooo extra that day," Zee said, rolling her eyes.

"What did Archie perform?" Ally asked.

"He wasn't there!" Zee said.

"What? That's strange."

"Yup, bailed at the last minute. But that's Archie. Unpredictable."

"Why didn't he show?"

"I don't know," Zee said. "He texted me congratulations last night, and when I asked him where he was or why he didn't perform, he never responded."

"Whaaaaat?" Chloe said, leaning back in her desk chair, putting her hand under her chin. "So what now?"

"You know, finding those old lyrics in my old Beans songbook made me wonder if the three of us should start writing songs again virtually. There's no reason we shouldn't keep creating music together just because we're apart," Zee said.

"That's true," Chloe said.

"How's therapy going?" Ally asked.

"Oh right, I meant to tell you. Dr. Banks was at the Festival. And get this, her husband is just as gorgeous as she is."

"Really?! What's his name? Let's Google him," Chloe said.

"Tyler Banks. Looks like that guy from that movie we saw at The Grove before I left."

"Whoa," Chloe said. "This guy?" She held up her phone to the computer screen.

Ally's eyes grew wide. "Whoaaaaa. Is he French?"

"Yes, super sleuth, that's him. And, no Ally, pretty sure he's British. "

Chloe shared the photo to the Zee Files. "Wow. He's Michael B. Jordan dad-hot."

"Seriously!" Zee said. "Like Michael B. Jordan as James Bond dad-hot."

"Dr. Banks has it all," Chloe said. "Career, husband, great fashion."

"Is there anything wrong with her?" Ally said.

"Nope," Zee said. "Even Archie approves of her."

"Speaking of Archie, what happens now?"

"Actually, I think I'm going to hang out more with Jasper. I would have never gotten that song in order had it not been for him. And I miss him. Our last jam session was super fun."

"Jas, what a sweetheart," Ally said.

"Yes, indeed. Ally, how are things at home?"

"They're okay. My dad is working like mad, so I'm home fending for myself a lot. Or I stay late at school to work on the literary journal. But I've been making new friends at the coffee shop we went to."

"What's going on with the literary journal?" asked Zee.

"My editor wants me to write a regular piece on my expat life in each issue now."

"That's amazing!"

"Yeah, I'm going to focus it around my independence in Paris. Being that I'm always alone anyway, it could be a commentary on Parisian life while I'm sitting up in my room looking down at the Parisian streets below."

Silence hung over the call as the girls all sat and stared blankly ahead of them.

"Don't look so sad, girls, it's fine. A different perspective on Parisian living," Ally said.

"Right," Chloe said finally. "On that note, I have to head to soccer practice. I'll be around later tomorrow. Zee, don't forget to ask about your photo from Izzy."

"Yes, ma'am," Zee said. "Bye!"

· · ·

Zee had just gotten back to school as her father barely pulled out of the campus carpark when the text came in. *Tea today?* It was from Archie, and it was short and to the point.

She hadn't heard from him since a few days before the Festival.

Zee

> Hello to you too. Good to see you haven't been kidnapped.

Archie

> Hi, Cali. Very funny. So, tea?

She had some time before dinner to change and meet up with him at Moe's Coffee Shop, and no plans except to study.

Zee

> Sure.

The campus was quiet—many students were still on their way back to campus from home, and those who were around were hanging out indoors. The chilly fall air felt like ice cubes on Zee's face, though she layered a T-shirt and ribbed tights under her gray turtleneck and leggings for the colder weather.

She grabbed both sides of her oversized varsity jacket and brought them tightly around her, walking faster to keep warm.

Moe's was busy with a few Hollows students either studying or hanging out, and locals enjoying their coffee and assortment of baked goods. The table by the window was free, so Zee placed her backpack on one chair and sat down at the seat facing the street. She took a breath, smoothed a hand over her hair, and let out a sigh.

Then Zee had a thought. *Is this a date?*

Zee smoothed her hands over her hair once again and put on another layer of her Charlotte Tilbury lip gloss, just in case.

"Cali," Archie said over her shoulder. She straightened up at the sound of his voice. "Sorry, I had to clean up after rugby. You look lovely as always." He looked over at the bar, where the special of the house, the turmeric latte, jumped out from the menu. "Those are proper, right? Do they have those back in California?"

"Pretty sure they do," Zee said. "But these are my local favorite."

"Right," he said. His mouth stretched into a warm smile.

"Are you getting one?" she asked.

"I might. You want one? I'll get them. Be right back."

He went to the register to order a drink. *He's buying the drinks. So it is a date*, Zee thought. She smoothed her hands over her hair one more time.

A few minutes later, Archie returned to their table with a nine of diamonds playing card on a long stick. "They'll bring them over when they're ready," he said.

"So why didn't I see you during the Festival?" Zee asked.

"Because I wasn't there," he said.

"But you had a song all written and everything. You were scheduled to perform as of last week. And then you just bailed."

"I wasn't here on Friday," Archie said. "I had to go to with my parents to Sweden on business." A server delivered two oversized cups of frothy golden-colored milk to their table and took away the playing card.

"These look delicious. Thank you," Zee said. Then she turned her attention back to Archie. "So you had to go to Sweden."

"Yeah," he said, sipping his latte. "My uncle is there, and my dad has some business to do. We met up with my cousins for the weekend. Pretty fun."

"Then how did you see my performance?" Zee asked.

"My mate sent me a video," Archie explained. He grabbed his cell phone from his pocket. "And Miss Izzy Matthews had the highlights up on her Instagram by the end of the night. She put most of it on her YouTube channel too. It was hard to miss you, Cali. You were the most popular performer."

I should really tune into Izzy's YouTube channel more often, Zee thought. Archie pulled up Izzy's channel and turned the phone horizontally. There it was, Izzy's latest video posted this morning. She had included a clip of Tom's spoken word performance, Jameela floating across the stage during her dance, and then Zee singing the chorus of her song. The camera then flipped back to Izzy and Poppy dancing to the song together, pumping their fists and bobbing their heads.

"Aww," Zee said. "Wow, I'm, like, touched."

"You're also, like, a music video now," Archie said. "Since she's posted the Festival video she's gotten nearly 75,000 followers. Soon the entire world will now know how great Zee Carmichael is. Remember me when you're famous?"

Zee laughed. "But what about your song?" she asked, leaning toward Archie.

"Oh that was just for you, Cali," Archie said. "I save the good stuff for you."

Zee looked away from Archie, blushing. "All those jam sessions we had, and you had no intention of playing it at the Festival?"

"Nah," he said. "Just wanted to check out your talent. And, you know, get to know you."

Zee nodded slowly. Archie smiled and raised his eyebrows.

"So will you play me more songs in the future?" Zee asked.

"Of course," he said, finishing off his latte. "C'mon, let's take a walk."

Zee gathered her things and stood up from table, and Archie held her chair out for her and tucked it back in as she stepped away. He let her walk in front of him toward the exit, then opened the door for her. They walked back to campus as the sun started to dip lower in the gray fall sky.

"Cali, you know more about me than anyone on campus," Archie said.

"Really?"

"I mean I have friends, mainly rugby buddies, but no girlfriends."

"I have noticed that," Zee said. "Though I'm sure any girl on campus would die to be your friend."

Archie laughed. "Well, I don't want any girl to be my girlfriend. I want you to be my girlfriend."

Zee stopped walking. She shook her head. "I'm sorry, what did you say?"

"Traffic's not that loud, Zee. You heard me right. I want

you to be my girlfriend."

Zee blinked. *What is happening right now?* she thought to herself.

"Listen, I feel comfortable around you. You make me happy. I like talking to you. What more could I want from a girlfriend?"

"I, um..." Zee stammered. "I don't know. I've never been someone's girlfriend."

"Well, it's the same thing as what we've been doing, except we'll hang out more and I won't have to beg you to have a latte or come with me to a show anymore."

Beg? Sending a few text messages asking what's up was begging? Zee thought.

"Um, okay," Zee said. "So that would make you my boyfriend?"

"Yeah, Cali," Archie said stepping closer to her. "That work for you? Means I'll never miss one of your gigs again."

Zee smiled. "Until you get another invite to Sweden with your family."

"Next invite to Sweden I get, you'll come with me."

Like my parents would ever agree to that, Zee thought to herself.

Archie stood in front of her, their faces close enough that he could see every freckle on her rosy cheeks. "So, are we?"

Zee shrugged her shoulders. "Sure."

Archie kissed her on the lips. The tender, pillow-soft mouth of Archie Saint John felt firmer and less sloppy than the mushy kisses her eighteen-month-old brother Connor gave her. Zee felt a fluttering in her chest, then her whole body felt like it was fluttering right off the ground.

After what seemed like an entire evening, Archie pulled away from Zee. "Great," he said. Zee opened her eyes. *Nope, I wasn't dreaming*, Zee thought.

"And as your boyfriend," Archie said, "I shall walk you back to your dorm like a true gentleman."

Archie extended his bent arm next to Zee, and she placed her hand in the crease of his elbow. Zee bit her lower lip. Her legs felt like jelly, but she leaned on Archie for support and walked in step with him. The chilly air whipped around them and tingled Zee's lips. The new couple walked hip to hip across the quad as Zee's chest fluttered with excitement and anxiousness. She was happy to be on the arm of Archie Saint John, but unsure about what the future has in store for her as Archie Saint John's girlfriend.

18

WHAT DOES IT ALL MEAN?

*Z*ee floated into her dorm room, still high from the kiss and kickstart to her formal relationship with Archie. *What in the world?* she thought. *How did this happen? Girlfriend. I'm Archie's girlfriend. I'm a real girlfriend, with a real boyfriend. Goodness.*

Zee had never been anyone's girlfriend. *What does that even mean?* she wondered. *What does that mean for my social life? Could I hang out with Jasper still? Do I have to call Archie every morning when I woke up? Will I go with him on international trips with his family? That part doesn't sound so bad, actually.*

I'll need to do some research, Zee thought, and went to her computer. She opened the browser and Googled "how to be a good girlfriend." A list of articles from popular women's magazines and websites popped up. The first one included a photo of a smiling girl with perfect teeth hugging her boyfriend around the neck. She was holding an oversized stuffed animal and the blurred lights from a merry-go-round could be seen in the background. Tips in the story included "shower him with compliments," "make friends with his friends," and "give him lots of space." *Space.* Zee thought. *I like space. I'm actually great at space.*

Another article, "Ten Ways to Level Up Your Girlfriend Game," listed some more actionable tips, like "show him affection in public" and "delight him by dressing up for date night." *Delight him by dressing up?! How about delight him with an amazing performance in front of thousands of people at the school's biggest show of the year? Oops... yup, did that already!*

Rolling her eyes, Zee quickly pulled up the Zee Files and left a message for the girls.

A few minutes later, a video chat request from Chloe popped up on Zee's computer. Zee clicked to accept, and the two began a video call.

"Wait. Archie disappears, comes back to campus, and makes you his girlfriend?" Chloe asked. "We just spoke yesterday and all of this has happened since?!"

"Yep!" Zee said. "I mean, I'm shocked too."

"Wow. That was fast! But then, not really. If you think about it, he's been pretty open with you the whole step of the way."

"Has he?" Zee thought aloud. "I mean, I guess he has. It's just crazy. Why would he be interested in me? He travels around the world on a whim. He has more money than the Bank of England!"

"Um, one, you're beautiful," Chloe said. "Two, you're the new girl from California, so you're a fresh face to him. And three, you're an awesome singer. Of course he wants to be with you."

"You are really my biggest cheerleader, Chlo," Zee said.

"It's all true! Plus, money still couldn't save him from therapy and what sounds like a lonely family life," Chloe said.

"Yeah, I guess," Zee said. "He just seems so..."

"What, sophisticated?"

"Yes?" Zee said. "It's just crazy that the people who you think have it all together are the ones who don't."

"Of course," Chloe said. "All that glitters isn't gold."

"What does that mean?"

"It means that just becomes something looks pretty or polished doesn't mean it always is."

Zee thought about what Chloe said. She thought about her school friends, whom she always perceived to be more mature than she was. Like Archie. Money and good looks haven't kept him from feeling lonely and sad. Jameela has perfect hair, perfect clothes, and a perfect turnout, but she, too, has her issues around dancing.

Jasper was exceptionally talented at mixing sound, but also extremely shy in front of a camera. *And then there's me,* Zee thought. *I'm struggling to find my place and meanwhile, Archie thinks I'm all shiny and glittery. What did he say about me again?*

"Yup, everyone's got something," Zee said.

"Well, I'm not saying to look for something bad in every person," Chloe said. "Just that those who you think have it all together oftentimes are struggling too."

"True. What's your thing?"

"I don't have one. I'm perfect." Chloe said.

An awkward silence fell between her and Zee.

"I'm kidding!" Chloe said. "For real, sleep is my thing. I'm not getting enough. I'm on the paper, I'm playing soccer, and I'm studying, and I crash at midnight every day and get up at 6 a.m. I'm tired all. The. Time."

"Why don't you take a break?" Zee said. "Or go to bed earlier?"

"I try, but my mind thinks about all the things I'm going to do or want to do. I can't help it."

"Oh boy," Zee said. "Well, it's Sunday afternoon there. Try and get some sleep. Hang up now and go back to bed."

"I still have to study though."·

"Study in bed. And text me after you've taken at least a two-hour nap, okay?"

"Deal. And keep me posted on your boyfriend. I can't believe you have a boyfriend. I can't believe you're the first of us to have a boyfriend!"

"I can't believe it either. But I know one thing," Zee said,

remembering back to the feeling she had walking across the quad. "First kisses are sweeeeet."

"Was it nice?"

"I... honestly can't describe it. Other than sweet."

"Goodness," Chloe sighed. "All right, sweet kisses to you, and sweet dreams to me. Off for a nap."

The two clicked out of the video call. Zee got up from her desk and plopped down in her bed. She closed her eyes for a few seconds to give her mind a chance to slow down from all of the day's events. Thoughts of Archie popped back into her mind and she smiled automatically. "Girlfriend," she said quietly to herself.

Zee opened her eyes and sat up in bed, feeling a buzz of energy in her body. She needed something to do besides daydream about Archie and that first kiss. She reached for her journal and began reflecting on all of the things that had happened in the past few days. Therapy. Festival. Archie.

She looked at the list of journal prompts from Dr. Banks she had folded up in between the middle of the book. She had made her way through a third of the list and now looked at the next one on there: *What is something that you're looking forward to?*

Zee looked up for a moment. That excited buzz of energy fired through her body again, and her mouth spread into another giddy smile. She wrote down the first thing that popped into her mind: *Figuring out what being Archie Saint John's girlfriend is really like.*

THE END

Read on to see what happens with Zee and her friends in Book 3 of The Zee Files, *Girl/Friend*.

1
ZEE'S BIG NEWS

The buzzing of the phone stirred Mackenzie "Zee" Blue Carmichael from a rare eight hours of sleep as she blearily looked at the screen. *Good morning, sleepyhead,* the text message read.

Archie Saint John used to send texts to Zee only in the evenings before lights out. But since they became officially girlfriend and boyfriend, he texted her every morning, first to say "Good morning," then to ask, "Did you dream about me?" and finally "Let's get breakfast." At first, Zee thought the sweet messages were cute. Then she wondered for how long and how many messages would keep coming.

With one eye open, Zee tapped out a reply. *Morning. You're up early.* She put the phone back down on her nightstand and turned over for a few more minutes of sleep.

The phone buzzed again a few seconds later. *I woke up thinking about you,* Archie quickly responded. *Shall we get breakfast this morning together?*

Zee sighed. She looked up at the ceiling in her dorm room at The Hollows Creative Arts Academy, the premier creative arts boarding school in the U.K. Then she turned toward her roommate Jameela Chopra's bed, which was already made up with the comforter smoothed out and the pillows carefully arranged.

Zee thought back to the last time she ate breakfast alone, with her roommate, or with anyone else besides Archie. When was the last time she had a message on her phone that wasn't from Archie? She wondered if she'd ever have a morning to sleep in, to journal and write, to eat whatever she wanted for breakfast and not have an audience of Archie Saint John watching her every move. But now there was little time for daydreaming, because she had to get herself presentable for her fourth breakfast date of the week. Zee tossed back her blanket, got out of bed, and headed for the shower. She let out a big breath. *Being a girlfriend is a full-time job,* she thought.

It had been less than a week since Archie asked Zee to be his girlfriend. She had kept the news under wraps, except for telling her best friends Chloe Lawrence-Johnson, who lived back in California, and Ally Stern, who lived in Paris. Zee couldn't keep anything from them. She had texted the girls the same night Archie kissed her and asked her to be BF/GF, and for the next couple days she had sent a flurry of texts and posted messages to the Zee Files, the private file and messaging system the girls had created to keep in touch with each other across continents and time zones. Zee uploaded pictures and screengrabs of Archie's texts to the file, like a photo of the turmeric latte they always ordered at Moe's Coffee Shop on Main Street. She also uploaded a selfie of Archie and her together in front of the dorm two nights ago. It was their first picture together as a couple.

After returning from the shower, Zee saw Archie had sent two more messages. *Meet you at 7:30 for breakfast?*

It was 7:15 a.m.

Yes? Archie followed up when Zee didn't respond immediately.

Yes, she replied, hurrying to get dressed. Zee fixed her hair into a tidy ponytail, her red curly hair cascading down her back, and put on a smear of highlighter on each cheek, just to look a little fresher to meet up with her new boyfriend.

Jameela, looking ready for a full day of classes dressed in her crisply ironed Misha Nonoo uniform jacket, a white button-down shirt, and a navy pleated skirt, walked into their shared bedroom to grab her books for the day. "Morning," she said.

"Good morning," Zee replied.

"Busy day ahead?"

"Class, study hall, a little soccer. You?"

"The usual. Class, dance, dinner. I've got to pick up something at the ballet studio before I go to class. Are you heading to breakfast?"

"Yes, but I'm going to have breakfast with Archie."

"Archie, Archie, Archie," Jameela said. "I haven't seen you in a couple of days because I've been so busy with studies and dance and everything. Correct me if I'm wrong, but you seem to be spending a lot of time with Mr. Archie Saint John, is that right?"

Zee pursed her lips. It was impossible to hide the truth about her and Archie any longer. "I guess I hadn't told you yet," Zee said. "Archie and I are boyfriend and girlfriend."

Jameela brought her hand to her chest. Her eyes widened and her mouth dropped. "Excuse me? You and Archie are what now?"

"Yes, Jameela," Zee said, smoothing her hair. "He asked me to be his girlfriend a few days ago. We've been together since."

Jameela looked at Zee, her eyebrows raised. "Like, *together* together?"

"Yes."

"Like, you two have kissed?"

"Yes, nosy-pants, we have kissed."

Jameela rolled her eyes, her eyebrows up toward the ceiling. "Oh. My. Goodness. I can't believe it's happened. But I'm not surprised by the way that you two have been having these private meetups and jam sessions since you've arrived on campus."

Zee grabbed her backpack. "Music is something we're both passionate about, yes. But now that you mention it, we haven't worked on any music together since the Festival." The Hollows had just held its annual Creative Arts Festival, the biggest on-campus talent show of the year, and Zee had wowed the crowd with her debut performance.

"Speaking of music," Jameela said, "what does Jasper think about this new relationship?"

Jasper's opinion of her new relationship was one of the reasons Zee tried to keep the news under wraps. Jasper Chapman was Zee's closest guy friend, and she really valued his opinion. They first met when Jasper moved from London to California and attended Brookdale Academy with Zee. The two bonded quickly over their love of music, but he moved back home to London after a year. When Zee's family had planned to move to the U.K., her parents had enrolled Zee at The Hollows in part because Jasper was already attending there. Jasper was reliable, creative, and welcoming to most people. Except to Archie.

Jasper thought Archie was too standoffish to be a good friend, or anything else, for Zee. "He's just this privileged kid who gets away with murder because he has money," Jasper had said on more than one occasion. But Archie had opened up to Zee in ways he didn't open up to other people. And that special bond made a solid foundation for a relationship. At least that's what the magazines said, Zee thought.

"I don't know what Jasper thinks," Zee said. "He doesn't know yet."

"He doesn't?" Jameela said, surprised. "Isn't Jasper your best mate?"

"Yes, but you're my roommate and I'm just getting around to telling you."

"True," Jameela said. "This is what happens when I spend all of my time at the dance studio. I miss out on such important things. So does this mean you'll be having all of your meals with Archie now? Should I not wait for you for dinner?"

"No, that's not what it means. I'll still have dinner with you and Jas and Tom. I still have my own life," Zee said.

"I hope so," Jameela said. "I wouldn't want Archie to swoop in and then we never see you anymore."

"Don't worry, that won't happen."

"Right," Jameela said. She grabbed her backpack from the floor near her dresser. "I'm heading out. I definitely want to catch up later and hear more about your re-LAY-shun-sheep."

"Don't say it like that," Zee giggled.

"Well, that's what it is, isn't it?"

Zee let out a loud sigh. "I'll see you at dinner."

Acknowledgments

First, thank you to Tina Wells for tapping me to co-write *The Zee Files*. You trusted me with your darling Zee, and together we've given her a world of fun, creativity, and wonder. Plus, you've helped me achieve my own dream of writing children's fiction. Here's to many more years of friendship and creative collaboration.

To my husband, Eric, you've supported me through good times and in bad, and along the way showed me the sunnier side of life. Thank you for your patience and for your love. My life is better with you in it.

To my mother, Jeanette. My best friend, my hero, my biggest cheerleader. Thank you for always being there for me no matter how trivial or tremendous my needs. I would not be who I am today without your guidance. I love you.

To my father, Art. You will always be with me. I hope I'm making you proud in heaven. I miss you every day.

To Wendy, Tamika, BJ, Xavier, Julius, and my extended family, thank you for your love and support. I work every day to be the sister/cousin/niece you're proud of!

To Joan Pattarozzi, my dear friend and lawyer who I've known for more than half of my life. I love you and am so thankful to have you as a spiritual and legal confidante. To Claudia Batchelor and Scarlett, my "people in the U.K." I am so thankful for your guidance and support. Claudia, we miss you in DR. Please come back soon.

To Jennifer Newens, Olivia Ngai, and the entire team at West Margin Press, thank you for welcoming me to your family, and for the love you've shown *The Zee Files* through publication.

To Kate Udvari and the entire Target team, thank you for creating a happy home for *The Zee Files*. It's a blessing to work with such a wonderful group of people.

To my many friends in New York, Dominican Republic, and around the world, thank you for being in my life. Your presence helps feed my soul every day.

To the readers of *The Zee Files*, thank you for tuning in and reading every word on these pages. I am so thrilled to be a part of your world.

—Stephanie Smith